Gypsy

by

Michael Walsh

A Matt Conley Mystery

Gypsy

Cover Art by *Diana Carlile*

The Wild Rose Press, Inc.
PO Box 708
Adams Basin, NY 14410-0708
Visit us at www.thewildrosepress.com

Publishing History
First Mainstream Mystery Edition, 2017
Print ISBN 978-1-5092-1207-1
Digital ISBN 978-1-5092-1208-8

A Matt Conley Mystery
Published in the United States of America

"What do they want?"

"A girl was murdered nearby," he said. "It's about her."

She sank back on her haunches and waved him in. He climbed inside, into humid air. Her shoulder touched his and he felt heat and firmness through her gossamer blouse. When she closed the door and made him part of her private space, he suddenly felt surprisingly comfortable in the small space. Maybe even—welcome? More likely it was wishful thinking. God knew welcome wasn't a sensation he felt much at home any more.

The woman bent toward a wooden box and her leg brushed his.

"What do you want, Mr. Policeman?" she asked, and opened an ornate cigar box whose top had *La Corona* printed in gold letters. A sweet, smoky scent filled the van.

"I want to help. I also apologize for my partner. He shouldn't have attacked your…?"

"Grandfather."

"Your grandfather. I hope he'll be all right."

"He will."

"I also need to talk with the man who threw the knives. Where was he last night?" Conley felt compelled to touch the old man. His skin felt like paper.

"My brother Luca was here with me," she said and reached into the box. When she withdrew her hand the fingertips glistened. She caressed the ragged cut on the old man's temple with the clear liquid and ran her fingers the length of the wound. Two more passes and the cut was gone, erased.

Praise for Michael Walsh

"[*OCEAN PARK* is for] mystery fans who value talent and originality."

~The Vine Voice

Dedication

For my wife Jean,
my partner in everything.

Part 1

Ocean Park

Chapter One

The young cop's nametag read Dunion. The spray of freckles across his cheeks and nose matched the color of his eyes—eyes that refused to look where his trembling finger pointed.

"End of the knoll," he said to Detective Matt Conley and his partner Danny Angelo. "In the pine grove."

A white mass showed through the pines, an unnatural color, an affront to the bright May morning sky and the emerald forest in front of them. The knoll was a grassy fairway, the product of a depression-era work project that carved a public garden from Ocean Park's rambling forest, one of the largest municipal reservations in greater Boston. The lawn rose to the tree line in long steps, a half dozen rectangular plateaus.

Conley nodded and they set off. Angelo's wingtips whispered through the grass. His trousers had knife-edge creases and his starched cuffs settled on his shiny shoes like crowns. He turned twice, just a twitch of the neck, to show displeasure at Conley's lagging.

Conley smiled. His wife Lisa was amused by Angelo's penchant for neatness, his obsession with order and discipline. They'd met only a few times, at the department Christmas party and monthly dinners. When she was sober—a rare occurrence these days—she'd often comment on Angelo's dress and demeanor.

He's always trying to be perfect, isn't he? It's not normal, Matt. He tries way too hard.

They climbed the plateaus. Conley pictured a burly Irish foreman barking orders to an army of immigrants who wore suspenders and scally caps, and battled with picks and shovels, wondering why they were building steps only a giant could use.

Almost there. The white grew. A sudden gust teased the branches of the twin pines that waved in welcome. The wind carried the rich, earthy smell of nature, along with something else. The sound of water moving across rocks murmured from the opening. Blowing branches hid the white thing now. Angelo parted the pine boughs with his hand.

A girl lay in a fetal curl on a small rise next to a meandering brook. She was naked, her skin as soft-looking as the ferns that made her bed. Her folded hands formed a pillow like a sleeping child's. An ugly color circled her neck, a tattoo blue, and sticks protruded from her eyes—crooked, twisting branches.

Angelo retrieved a notebook from his coat pocket and spoke. "What do you see?"

Conley crossed the water and skirted the body, placing his feet carefully. He put on a plastic glove and touched her cheek. "Body's neither stiff nor swollen. She hasn't been here long."

Angelo scribbled.

"Young, maybe twenty," Conley continued. "No visible weapons at the scene."

"Except the sticks."

The sticks.

Conley looked up and saw the yellow insides of the tree branches they'd come from. Maybe a pang of conscience was convincing the killer to spare her, so it was easier to reach up, snap off a twig, and put an end to those pleading eyes. Easier than letting her go.

Voices carried from the bottom of the glen. Others had joined Dunion, and two crime scene techs were walking toward them.

Back to the girl. Theories and musings weren't something Angelo cared to record in his leather-bound book. He'd complained about that often enough. He wanted facts, not dark movies that played in the mind—those brought scorn and scolding. Since Chief of Detectives Ray Kerrigan had announced his retirement, Danny Angelo had stepped up his game. It was well-known Angelo wanted the job, and he tolerated no nonsense in his pursuit.

Conley described the victim's thick black hair, unblemished skin, lean body. He sounded like her lover—until he described the eyes and neck.

The techs were almost there, lugging heavy bags.

A hummingbird fought through a thicket nearby. It escaped, bulleting past his head, and a flurry of its lost feathers floated to a crooked path. He left Angelo to his notebook and followed the trail, a mulch of broken pinecones and rotting leaves. The path wound through dense forest and opened on a rose garden, more of FDR's busywork. He walked through a shower of sweet scents and stopped at a road made of gravel and ruts.

On the other side loomed a modest, sun-dappled hill. An old man stood near the top, a canvas sack slung over his shoulder like a paperboy's. He shimmered and Conley realized the shine came from an earring under the man's porkpie hat.

Movement behind. Angelo was suddenly at his

shoulder. "Gypsy," he said.

"What's he doing?"

"Foraging."

Conley had never seen a Gypsy, except in picture books. *Campfires and tambourines. Bandanas and fortune telling.*

"A carnival came to town last week," Angelo said. "Bunch of them camped down by the lake."

"What's he looking for?"

"Roots, berries, herbs. For potions."

Potions. The idea intrigued. Potions for love, potions to cure disease, maybe a potion that carried a curse—or lifted one.

"Damn Gyps," Angelo said, and Porkpie Hat disappeared over the hill. Angelo stepped ahead, staring at the place where the old man had been. "Let's sweat 'em."

They crossed the rutted dirt road and stood at the bottom of the hill. Steeper than it looked from afar.

"Maybe we should follow the road and go around," Conley said.

"You can," Angelo replied and climbed. Long grass wrapped his legs and pulled at his trousers. When he reached scrub bushes, he clutched their tops and used them as handholds. Clouds hid the sun, and shadow sucked the vibrant green from the hill's foliage, turning it brown and gray. In his shiny black suit, he looked like a mistake in the middle of an antique photo. Past the bushes, he leaned forward, hands touching ground as he trucked upward. He'd chosen a poor path, but he'd never admit such a thing.

Stubbornness, thy name is Angelo.

The old Gypsy hadn't climbed straight, he'd

walked the hill at an angle, tacking back and forth. Conley did the same—trekking sideways and doing about-face turns, crossing behind his partner.

Angelo's flat-soled street shoes skidded backward and he slid to a knee. He righted himself, his trousers sporting a streak of green. They reached the top together, Angelo panting, palms pressed against his sides. The sun had returned and shone on a circle of cars, campers, and trucks below, creating sparkles that gave the appearance of a giant necklace laid on the ground. Pine trees lined the space beyond, roots anchored in the sparse soil between rocks and small cliffs bordering the lake. The water was so still it looked frozen.

Angelo shook a Camel from his pack, slipped it between his lips, lit up, and gazed at the sky—the signal he was about to be expansive. Lately, Lisa had been the object of his unsolicited guidance. Conley could guess his partner's next words.

Go home to your wife, Conley, she needs you. Lisa's a good woman, going through a hell you and I can't imagine.

Thanks for the tip, but I don't need encouragement, especially from you. My every available minute is spent nursing Lisa back to sobriety, and to the happiness we once had. We'll be whole again soon. Very soon.

But liquor wasn't the only problem. Lisa had cheated on him, had broken her vows, and the infidelity had changed their relationship. Her betrayal was something he'd learned to forgive, but would never understand. Matthew Conley didn't break promises.

Surprisingly, Angelo didn't talk about Lisa this time. He directed his wisdom toward the dead girl, and waved his lit cigarette at the Gypsy camp.

"They know something," he said. "I feel it. They know who raped and killed that poor kid."

"How do you know he raped her?"

Angelo shrugged. "Why wouldn't he? These Gypsy animals probably did it—raped her, killed her, mutilated her." His eyes squinted from the smoke. "And I ain't entirely sure I stated the order of those three events correctly."

A rustle below. The old Gyp was halfway down the hill.

"Hey!" Angelo yelled and snapped his cigarette to the ground.

The old man added something to his canvas bag, lifted his head to the new day, and ambled toward the camp.

Angelo stepped off the rise. "Hey asshole, I'm calling you!"

No response.

Conley stamped out the cigarette and followed. The hill was even steeper on this side, and each step felt like the beginning of flight, as if a proper wind current could float them to the bottom. Angelo seemed to find a rhythm, two steps and a leap, until he stumbled through a pile of dried leaves that crackled like paper and clung to him. He cursed, stood straight, and surfed in dirt before he fell. He sat and rose in one motion, ending up covered with dirt and leaves. Conley had seen his partner's anger often enough—his red face and blazing eyes were signs that Angelo had gone nuclear. The old man was near the bottom of the hill now, close to the camp. Two large oaks formed the gateway he walked through.

A final command, a hoarse "STOP!" from Angelo. They were only feet apart.

Angelo reached the man and drove the heel of his fist between Porkpie Hat's shoulder blades. The old man fell forward and his bag emptied in midair, mushrooms flying and tumbling alongside his rolling hat. Roots and twigs spun in the air and rained on his back. Conley ran to help and put his hand on the old Gyp's arm. He suddenly turned, his face feral, and threw powder—a dusty, foul-smelling ash—into the air. Conley shook his head and rubbed his eyes as red dust settled on his head and shoulders.

A thwack sounded overhead, a sharp bite. A knife had dug into one of the trees, halfway to the hilt. Another one followed and Angelo dove onto the ground.

Conley drew his Glock. An old pickup with a rusted camper top sat on the other side of the clearing. A man in jeans and a gray T-shirt stood next to it, poised, holding another knife overhead. Conley fired a warning shot into the lake and the explosion echoed.

Angelo propped himself on an elbow. "Shoot the bastard, Conley."

Conley leveled his gun at the knife thrower's chest. The man was so dark he blended into shadows. His hair was as black as the char in the campfire between them. "I'll shoot if he moves."

"By then I'll have a blade in my back. Shoot him now, you moron. He tried to kill me."

"I don't think so, Angelo. Look at those knives. They're an inch apart. He hit what he aimed for."

Doors opened and closed, clicks and slams. Gypsies came from their campers, curious and groggy.

7

Children stood in baggy pajamas, and mismatched tops and bottoms. Women in sweatpants and faded housecoats pointed and chatted excitedly. No bandanas, no flowing dresses, just the clothes of everyday people. They watched Conley with sleepy almond eyes. No tambourines, no music, only the sound of Angelo's running commentary.

"Straight-haired niggers, that's what they are," Angelo said, still lying on the ground, his hair hanging over his eyes.

Gun against knife. Conley wondered how they'd break the push. He studied everything around him, every movement. "Liars," Angelo said. "Thieves. Kill that sonofabitch."

A unicorn was painted on the side of a van, galloping across a royal blue sky, past five-pointed stars and a lemon-slice moon.

"Shoot, damn it."

A fish jumped in the lake and the ripples spread.

"Kill him!"

A young woman broke from the crowd and circled the campfire. Cream-colored nightgown, same-colored skin. She came closer. Conley blinked twice, three times, not because his eyes were still clouded with dust, but because of a sight that could not be. The girl looked familiar—too familiar—the way her auburn hair fell off her shoulder, the way she carried herself, slender neck straight, head held high exactly like his wife. The girl looked—no, she *was* Lisa—a twin, but younger. Teenage Lisa—thin, lithe as a cat, skin glowing as if stoked by a furnace.

She passed the knife thrower in silence and walked in front of Conley's gun fearlessly as he marveled at the likeness. She knelt next to the old man, cradled his head, wiped blood from his cheek with her sleeve, and rested her palm on his forehead. His eyes widened and he said, "Gina."

Her face was turned away, but the voice Conley heard talking to him was a dream, the resurrection of a forgotten sound. The resemblance was impossible.

"You're brave enough to frighten an old man. Do you have the courage to lower the gun?"

His gun felt heavy, his mind confused. How could he have held his arm raised for so long—and let his weapon be pointed, even momentarily, at the woman he'd been madly in love with since the day they'd met? He turned the Glock sideways and balanced it loosely on his palm, studying it, suddenly struck by its strangeness.

"No!" Angelo barked. "No."

Conley lowered the gun.

Chapter Two

Conley holstered his Glock.

Massachusetts State Police cruisers were hurtling into the Gypsy camp, sirens blaring, flashers painting the forest blue. Spinning tires cut dark scars in the soft earth and sprayed mulch in waves. The cars stopped at angles, blocking the entrance to the clearing. Angelo scrambled to his feet. The Gypsies scattered and disappeared into campers and cars.

Troopers stepped out of the cruisers, unfolded their big bodies, and stood as straight and still as the oaks and elms around them. The plastic visors of their peaked caps shaded their faces. Sam Brown belts, slashes of leather from left shoulder to right hip, strained to hold muscular torsos. All at once they advanced toward Conley and Angelo, and the motion of their shined jackboots made their motoring legs look like machines.

Captain Roland Gerard, the Troop A Commander, led them. He stopped in front of Conley and Angelo.

"You boys left a body back there."

Conley glanced toward Angelo and tried to shrug the lapel of his jacket farther over his gun.

"The techs were with her," Angelo said suddenly, swinging his arm. "We saw a citizen nearby and followed him to interrogate."

Gerard studied Angelo, swung his face toward

Conley, and stared at the part of his gun that still showed. "You shoot this citizen, Conley? I heard a shot."

Angelo stepped between them. "Fuck off, Gerard. This is Ocean Park's case. We were first at the scene."

"I'm painfully aware of that, Detective Angelo. Techs said you destroyed footprints at the site." Gerard's voice resonated through the woods, in accusation, in judgment. "You're already hurting the cause."

"Get bent. This is a city case until the District Attorney decides otherwise. Chief Kerrigan's in charge."

Gerard raised his face toward the sun and smiled. His bald white head was clean-shaven, and even the back of his neck was hairless, with only a smudge of black and white stubble.

"At oh-seven-hundred hours this Wednesday morning the Essex County DA entrusted this investigation to the Massachusetts State Police." He shook his head, still smiling, still enjoying the sun. "Good man, that District Attorney."

Gerard raised the index fingers of both hands and pointed at the Gypsy vehicles as if firing imaginary pistols. His men fanned out. Their boots scissored and swung like metronomes. They walked to campers and trucks, and banged heavy fists on metal doors.

Gerard followed. Angelo yelled at his back. "First responders stick with the case as advisors. That's protocol."

"Protocol," Gerard drawled. "I hate that word." He turned his head slowly. "And those who use it."

****

Angelo followed Gerard, still cursing. Troopers approached the vehicles and knocked on windows and doors, a syncopated, echoing clatter. Taps, bangs, pounds. Their deep voices boomed. Angelo seethed.

Conley circled the campfire. Brave man, his partner Angelo. Downed a defenseless old man, then bitched and complained when he himself was thrown to the ground. That was life with Angelo, hypocritical rants followed by one angry gripe after another. His predictable partner would probably accuse the knife thrower of murdering the girl in the glen, and history proved Angelo wasn't above railroading an innocent man into a long stretch in Massachusetts' notorious Cedar Junction Prison. The young Gyp's arrest and prosecution would be a delicious mix of revenge and achievement that Danny Angelo could not resist.

Gypsy children watched. A dog with matted hair and a scar across an eye barked but kept its distance.

Conley walked to the unicorn van—*was drawn to the van*—and stood next to the painting of the bright creature flying through dark blue sky. He hunched against the side door, head down, and slapped his hand on the cold metal. The girl in the van would surely lead him to the knife thrower.

After a long wait, the latch clicked and the door slid sideways, a soft, squealing whir on a track. Gina appeared—*no, Lisa*—almond skin and liquid eyes just inches away. She was kneeling on a worn carpet whose frayed edges curled over the metal track and spiraled toward the ground. The old man lay on a thin mattress behind her. His eyes grew.

Conley raised his hands in a show of peace.
Or a plea for forgiveness?

A weak dome light shone in the middle of the ceiling, highlighting the colorful afghan that covered the man. His pale face was bone white.

Gina looked past Conley at the army that had invaded, and when she spoke her breath was warm and odorless.

"What do they want?"

"A girl was murdered nearby," he said. "It's about her."

She sank back on her haunches and waved him in. He climbed inside, into humid air. Her shoulder touched his and he felt heat and firmness through her gossamer blouse. When she closed the door and made him part of her private space, he suddenly felt surprisingly comfortable in the small space. Maybe even—welcome? More likely it was wishful thinking. God knew welcome wasn't a sensation he felt much at home any more.

The woman bent toward a wooden box and her leg brushed his.

"What do you want, Mr. Policeman?" she asked, and opened an ornate cigar box whose top had *La Corona* printed in gold letters. A sweet, smoky scent filled the van.

"I want to help. I also apologize for my partner. He shouldn't have attacked your…?"

"Grandfather."

"Your grandfather. I hope he'll be all right."

"He will."

"I also need to talk with the man who threw the knives. Where was he last night?" Conley felt compelled to touch the old man. His skin felt like paper.

"My brother Luca was here with me," she said and

reached into the box. When she withdrew her hand the fingertips glistened. She caressed the ragged cut on the old man's temple with the clear liquid and ran her fingers the length of the wound. Two more passes and the cut was gone, erased.

Like it never was.

"Are you sure he didn't leave?"

"Yes." She screwed the lid onto the open jar in the box. "Trust me, Mr. Policeman—if you're capable of it."

Trust—a word he and Lisa had struggled with for years. Angelo would scoff at the idea of it; he'd say Gypsies were masters of lying and deception. But the girl's intense, sincere eyes assured Conley her word was a precious thing.

He sensed a presence in the darkness and turned. The knife thrower crouched in the corner, arms wrapped around his knees. Their eyes locked. Points of light reflected off the knives on the floor beside him.

She rummaged in the cigar box again, and this time her fingertips carried a blue paste. She spread the substance on the moaning man's forehead, cheeks, nose, covering jaw, chin, and lips, and the paste glistened.

A sharp knock sounded on the outside of the van, and they froze. A second knock, fast and hard.

Conley slid the door open, squinting into sunlight and the hard, fresh face of a young trooper. The kid's bent knuckles were poised to knock again.

"Matthew Conley," he said, presenting his Ocean Park Detective badge. "I got this one," he said quickly and pulled against the door to shut it. The trooper's upturned fist unfolded and he wrapped his fingers around the edge of the door to stop its slide.

Conley positioned himself to hide the figure in the corner. The statie eyed Gina, then the old man.

"What's wrong with him?" he said, pointing his smooth chin at the old Gyp.

"I don't know yet. I'll share my report with Gerard," Conley lied.

The kid licked his lips and glanced across the clearing at his captain.

"No. I need to talk with everyone in the van."

The old man coughed and raised his hand, fingers fluttering toward the newcomer. He lifted his head. The blue paste shone like a mask.

"The geezer's sick," Conley said. "Might be typhoid."

The young cop froze and studied him. Conley knew what the kid was looking for—a blink, a twitch, a weakness. He held still.

And Conley knew what Gerard would do—with Angelo's urging—if he discovered the young Gyp who had a bad disposition and a fondness for knives. He'd introduce him to a sharp come-along that dug deep into wrists, a police car, and the basement of the Lewis Street Jail. There he'd meet fists, boots, maybe rubber hoses. And if the investigation dragged on, a confession signed under any circumstances would fend off the DA and reporters for a while. Why not? After all, the Gyp was surely guilty of something.

Aren't we all?

Seconds passed. When it was right, as if the proper number of beats had been silently drummed, Conley repeated, "I'll share my report with Gerard."

The trooper's hand dropped away. Conley slid the

door past the stone face.

Darkness again. They waited until the voices outside stopped, engines started, and tires crunched the carpet of branches and leaves.

The knives on the floor no longer shone. The light from the dome made twin white pinpoints in Gina's worried eyes. She closed the cigar box. "Pura," she whispered, and pressed the old man's hand between hers.

Conley shuddered at the vibrant, earnest sound of her voice, a forgotten memory—a delicious relic from his past.

Chapter Three

"Menagerie," Gina whispered on the day she turned eight years old.

She loved that word, loved the way it stretched and purred like a big cat.

"Menagerrrrrrie."

Pura lifted her onto his shoulders with his hard, strong hands and they visited animals under the big white tent on the winter circus grounds in Sarasota. When she squinted, the bars on the cages seemed to disappear, and she imagined getting close enough to pet the animals and stroke their fur. But Pura said their tongues were sandpaper, too rough for a little girl's soft face and hands.

Lion roared. She smiled and waved. When the cat showed teeth, Pura said he was smiling. Happy. She forced her lips high and low, and bared her teeth in greeting.

They moved on to Bear. He looked comfortable in his big brown coat. She'd miss him the most. She'd miss everything about menagerie, even the scratchy hay and the strong smells.

Pura set her down and stopped to inspect the yoke on one of the painted cages. She approached Bear. He opened a sleepy dark eye.

"Wake up, lazy bones," she said, and his wet nose fluttered and he growled without showing teeth.

The feeders marched into the big tent with buckets of red meat and pale fish, and the animals paced their cages and called hello to breakfast. When the men opened the cage doors, the animals roared. The fish and meat slapped loudly on the metal floors and her friends stood and pranced—even the sleepyheads—and ate noisily with very bad manners.

She wished she could be the feeder instead of these angry men who poked the animals through the bars with long sticks, teased them, and threw fish at their heads, as if it was their fault they couldn't go out and find food in the jungle.

She followed behind the ugly men, reminding Bear and Lion to watch their manners, and to eat quietly and slow.

Meanwhile, Pura was running his fingers over the bars, the wheels, the hitches, hunting for broken and loose parts. He had his toolbox with him, and that meant he'd be busy for a long time. The cages, the wheels, the hitches, he'd fix them all. He knew how to do everything in the circus, even knew how to shoe the white fairy-tale show horses.

She kissed him goodbye, waved to her friends, and left the cool tent to do her chores. The sun was getting warmer, making sweat beads on her forehead. The heat was a bad sign. Winter circus would be over soon and the trains would load tents, clowns, and acrobats, and head north. Sometimes she liked to pretend the coolness hadn't left.

Sadness lay ahead. Saying goodbye to friends until next year, goodbye to the children she and Luca played with, and the jugglers, roustabouts, and cooks. Goodbye to Officer Wesson, always laughing at the clowns practicing in the field.

She walked to the bay and picked shells from the white sand. She threw the broken ones far into the water so she wouldn't have to bother with them tomorrow. She collected the pretty ones, red and white fans and corkscrews, so she could glue them into pictures on the scrap boards Pura gave her. She created pictures of Lion raising his paw, Arabians trotting, Elephant trumpeting, and the townspeople eagerly bought them to remember the winter circus.

Across the harbor sat a pink house with its very own beach. A girl played on the sand, a thin girl with pale legs and blond hair. *Oh, to live like that,* Gina thought. To have her own beach, her very own treasure of shells, her very own home.

Someday.

The spiky shadows of palm trees followed her as she hunted, and she knew from their position her brother Luca would be awake now. She needed to feed sleepyhead. She stopped in the mess tent and loaded a bowl of cereal and a glass of milk on a tray.

Luca looked up when she came. He was kneeling, playing with blocks between the station wagon and the pop-up tent. She drew down the tailgate of the station wagon, unfolded a checkered tablecloth, and set the tray. He climbed up and ate.

She made the beds in the pop-up tent, and folded the blankets. Across the field Pura was coming toward her with his long lope. His legs always seemed disconnected from the rest of his body, like two thin, bending pipe stems that carried a belly, chest, smiling face, and fancy hat. One arm was at his side holding his heavy toolbox, and the other held sandwiches in wax paper. He'd come for lunch, but Luca hadn't even finished breakfast. Pura wouldn't be happy to know the boy had slept until noon.

She took Pura's lunch and spread it on the cloth next to the tray. He sat. Luca swung his legs. Pura slid his toolbox under the gate and turned to him.

"Good morning, Mr. Hollywood."

Luca's eyes opened wide and he made his silly expressions—big smile, sad frown, scary face.

Pura shared his sandwich with Luca and they ate quietly. When they were done, she poured tea for Pura. Her brother's face wore yellow mustard. She wet a napkin with water from a bottle and wiped his mouth.

"It's nice here, Pura," she said. "Salt air is good for us, that's what everyone says. And the sun feeds us vitamins. Right through our skin."

Pura worked his jackknife against his long fingernails, head down.

"We should stay here, Pura. When the circus goes, we should stay. Everyone says you're the best blacksmith and there's always work, even when the circus leaves."

Pura reached down to his box and rummaged through the tools. He ran his hand along the bottom, found something, and showed her. Three black nails lay across his palm. They had big round heads and the straight parts looked like carved wood. Sun shone on the dull nails, but they didn't shine back.

"Gina," he said, arm around her shoulder. His eyes looked cloudy. "When Jesus died, a blacksmith forged three nails for His cross."

She blessed herself at the mention of the Savior's name and started to tell her grandfather to do the same, but hesitated. Instead, she said, "I know. One for each hand, Pura, and one for both feet. A big nail."

"Do you know who that blacksmith was?" he said.

She shook her head and waited, still as she could make herself, for the answer.

"Rom."

"No, Pura," she whispered. "A Gypsy? A Gypsy helped kill Jesus?"

"God made a curse that day. He commanded the Rom to travel and learn like His son did. Travel and learn." He kissed her on the forehead. "God wills it. But like all curses, there's a lesson inside. A home can be a prison, Gina, and a house can crumble."

He dropped the nails in the toolbox and they clattered past the tools and settled on the bottom.

Didn't matter. She wanted a home, a pink house on the water so she could open a bedroom window in the morning and see sparkling water and white sand. She prayed to God to change His mind.

Shouts in the distance, in the mess tent. Officer Wesson threw the white entrance flap back and marched out to the field. A man followed, limping, trying to keep up with the policeman's long legs. He waved his arms like the clowns and barked at Officer like Sea Lion. The loud man looked like a misbehaving child —if not for his bald head and ugly beard. They came quickly across the field, mowing the long grass flat with their steps, swinging arms quickly, as if that somehow made them go faster.

Closer.

Pura stood. He lifted Luca and placed him in her arms.

Closer.

21

A feeder. She recognized the bald man as the one who fed Bear, the nasty man who poked him with sticks.

Officer Wesson stopped in front of them, arms still at his side. Bald Man stood behind and looked around his wide shoulder. Both were breathing loud from their march.

"We got ourselves a problem," Officer said to Pura.

She turned so Luca looked back at the circus.

"We got ourselves a thief is what we got," Bald Man said in a high voice. He poked his finger in the air toward her grandfather, just like he poked animals with the stick.

Pura spoke slowly. "I'm no thief, Wesson."

Officer nodded. "Well, we need to put that claim to the test, Pura. That we do."

He looked inside the window of the station wagon, drew his billy club from his belt, reached in the back, and knocked clothes and shoes onto the floor. Luca's toys clinked.

The feeder watched and waited. He looked at Gina and Luca with watery eyes and licked his lips like he was thirsty—or hungry.

Officer climbed in the car, messed her neat pile of clothes with his billy, and poked at Pura's cooking pots and Luca's picture books. Cracks sounded when he knelt on her bag of sea shells and the pictures she'd made. She imagined them dissolving to pink-white powder.

"Don't do this, Wesson," her grandfather said.

He called back and his voice sounded muffled, as if he were in a cave. "If you're clean, good luck to you,

Pura. You've nothing to worry about."

Bald man asked a question.

"Wesson, you Irish angel, have you found my money yet?"

Officer ignored him and moved to the pop-up tent, and his weight rocked and shivered their home. Blankets, sheets, and pillows were thrown onto the ground in a lump.

She loved Officer, but today he was acting like a bad cat, on all fours, clawing with his club as if it were a paw.

The commotion stopped. Bald Man took in a breath. Officer backed out of the tent with Pura's cigar box and opened it. Pura's jars glistened in rows. Photos of grandma, smiling, were taped to the top cover. A thick roll of money stood between the jars.

"Good work, Wesson," the feeder said. "You found my money."

Officer lifted the tight roll and held it on his palm like a prize.

Pura spoke.

"That's three months' wages, Wesson. I worked hard for that stake. Gina too."

"Three months of *my* wages, you thieving Gyp," Bald Man said as if spitting. His eyes seemed to pop from his head, but they weren't like the mostly white eyes of normal people. His had thin red bloodlines traveling the roundness like spiderwebs, and the black centers were as narrow as pencil tips. "Justice has been dispensed," he said. "Celebration's in order."

He reached for the money, but Officer held it back. He peeled off half the dollars, folded them, and stuffed the roll in his pocket.

Pura spoke, his lips hardly moving. "You've sinned, Wesson."

"Ah, an accusation from an expert."

Bald Man whispered, "This was my idea, Wesson. You have no right."

Officer said, "No right? What about taxes, Broderick? Consider yourself square with the local government."

Bald Man wiped his lips and squeezed the dollars in his fist. His eyes were narrow now, squinting, the wrinkled lids almost closed. He turned and hurried back toward the tents.

Officer shook his stick like a wagging finger.

"You be off tomorrow, Pura, you and your grandkids. It's time you took your magic elsewhere."

Luca cried louder. Gina didn't move. Pura stared at the policeman until Officer finally reached in his pocket and his hand came out with two of the bills. He held them high, let go, and they floated to the ground.

"A bit of charity for you, old man. Milk for the kids, gasoline to put distance between us. And some advice, Pura. Don't come back or you'll find a harsher type of justice."

Pura was arranging the jars in his box now, closing the cover slowly. Suddenly his hand darted to Officer's face, just a blur. There was a smear of green paste on his fingers, what her aunts called a dollop, and he wiped it on Officer Wesson's cheek. The policeman stepped back and rubbed the spot.

"Don't come back, Pura," he said again, louder, angry. He held the back of his hand against his face. The green was no longer on his cheek, it was in the skin like a tattoo, a picture of Pura's fingers, even the long fingernails. Soon the picture grew and spread. His face was turning the color of dollar bills.

"You'll not see us again, Wesson," her grandfather said, but no one seemed to be listening.

Luca sobbed. Gina hugged him harder.

Officer dropped his billy club. He was feeling his face with both hands now, fingertips touching nose, neck, forehead.

Pura smiled and waved his clean hand high in the air.

"But you'll have something to remember us by."

Chapter Four

A banshee cry—*Shrill—Unbridled.*

Lisa's shrieks followed Conley from room to room in their house on the Thursday before Memorial Day. He knelt, his knees grinding on cold tiles as he opened the cabinet under the vanity.

"Matthew!" she screamed from the bedroom.

Lisa was badly hungover. When he came home that evening, he'd found her in bed, pale and moaning, wrapped in sweat-drenched sheets. She'd gotten ahold of liquor despite his best efforts.

He brushed aside medicine bottles in the cabinet, gauze bandages, a heating pad and electrical cord. A puff of talcum powder, its scent clean and downy, escaped from a white plastic bottle and settled on his hand. He reached in every corner. Nothing. He whacked his head on the counter when he stood and returned to the hall. Which way?

Think!

Laundry room. Clothes were strewn on the floor, liquid soap gelled on top of the washer, and a hardened yellow icicle of dried soap hung on its side. The overhead fluorescent flickered like heat lightning, and thunder followed—

"Help me!"

I am.

He searched the clothes basket, through soiled

things, bunched and musty, and felt the smooth plastic bottom. Nothing here.

To the hall again.

Running out of places.

Kitchen.

A groan from the bedroom, a long gargled sound like strangling.

He opened the overhead cabinets, felt behind dishes and plates, brushed a glass, and it fell and shattered on the floor.

Footsteps shuffled behind him. Lisa appeared in the doorway and leaned against the jamb. Her face was drawn, her skin the color of putty, and her hair was matted to one side like an old-time movie star. The frayed bottom of her soiled robe brushed the tops of her pale bare feet.

Must be getting close. Through the refrigerator, then the freezer. A bag of frozen vegetables fell and landed on his feet with a crunch. Not there.

He stood in the middle of the kitchen and looked around, but not at her.

Few places left. He opened the oven and smelled the crusted, blackened pans. The light was out—or removed. He reached in the dark space and touched the sooty racks and greasy pans before he felt the smooth hardness of the bottle. He turned to her as he drew it out.

Gordon's gin, a half-empty soldier. His eyes locked on hers as he twisted the cap off, held the bottle high over the sink, and turned it sideways. Booze cascaded into the drain, splattering his clothes. A scent like pine needles filled the room.

Could she smell it?

She spoke.

"I'm so sorry, honey. I swear I won't touch a drop again," she said in a soft whisper that sounded like it might be powered by her final breath. "I swear to God."

****

The following morning, Conley sat in his car in the driveway, hands gripping the wheel at two and ten o'clock, exhaust billowing around him.

Angelo stopped his car at the curb, got out, marched up the driveway, and knocked on the driver's window. "Living in your car now, Conley?"

He rolled the window down. "Just thinking. I found Lisa's stash in the back of the oven."

"Congratulations. You're quite the detective."

"I'm going to make a list of her hiding places so I don't forget. Make it easier to find the booze next time."

Angelo shook his head. "That's not the answer, you know." His cheeks were rosy, his serious eyes like dark BBs.

"Certainly save time."

"Certainly save you from facing real problems."

He dropped the gear shift into reverse. "We lost a child several years ago—Brendan. Lisa tried to get over it with work and career and then…alcohol."

No need to mention the affair. For all Matt knew, Angelo might know about it already. The circles they ran in were small.

"Doesn't matter. If you make excuses, you'll get soft on her."

"I don't need your shit today, Angelo."

"If you don't get through to her," Angelo said slowly, "her liver will quit soon, or else the blood vessels in her throat will burst and she'll bleed to death. That's how most drunks die."

"How do you know so much?"

Angelo's eyes narrowed. "My father bled to death. I was just a kid when my grandfather drove him to the ER because my old man was choking on his own blood. I watched from the hospital hallway as they packed his throat with ice. The bleeding stopped for a while. Then the ice melted and he coughed pink water until he finally croaked. My mother felt sorry for him after he went bankrupt, and that was her mistake. He only drank more. She died from heart failure less than a year later, after months of blaming herself."

Angelo looked away for a moment, then back to Conley, his expression defiant. "So I know something about pity."

He'd worked with Angelo for a year and never learned anything about him, other than he was a pain-in-the-ass perfectionist with a nasty attitude. This revelation was the closest Angelo had ever come to sharing his personal life, and it ended abruptly.

"Let's go."

"Angelo, why didn't you say anything about the girl at the Gypsy camp?"

"Come again?"

"The girl—Gina—was a clone of Lisa. You had to see that. But you didn't say a word. Why?"

"A clone? What are you talking about, Conley? They were all greasers—"

"Her hair, her eyes—how could you have missed it?"

Angelo studied Conley's face for a ten-count. Birds twittered in the trees that hung over the driveway, a dog barked in the distance, and Angelo expressed his opinion. "You're an ass-wipe, pal. Tripping on some damn Gypsy 'cause you think she looks like your wife."

Angelo's phone rang. He turned, answered, and headed down the driveway. He shouted over his shoulder.

"C'mon, Conley, get in the car. We got work to do. Two days into this investigation and we don't have shit." He suddenly stopped and smirked. Somehow Angelo had the ability to make even a smile seem obscene. "But we can swing by their camp again if you want. Maybe the Gypsy bitch requires further inspection."

Chapter Five

The ceiling of St. Margaret's Church sported magnificent teak rafters, curved beams that looked like the ribs of an upside-down ark. The ceiling was bone white, the heating vents immaculate. The parishioners lining the back pews for Saturday penance, waiting for an open confessional, were mostly young, well-tailored, and patient. A stark contrast to the church Conley grew up in—the Church of St. Ambrose—which had been destroyed by fire. Its pastor, Father McCarrick, had reluctantly relocated with his parishioners to this modern place in the suburbs.

Conley's turn next. He entered the confessional, knelt on the kneeler, and sighed. He'd spent the day with Angelo interviewing neighbors near Ocean Park Woods, and his legs ached. The wooden divider rose with a *chock* and the dark silhouette of the priest on the other side of the ornate screen leaned toward him.

"Forgive me, Father, I've sinned."

Silence followed. The steady hum of circulating air filled the tiny space.

"Go on, be quick about it," McCarrick prompted. "I've got a lot of customers today."

"It's not that simple," Conley said. "I'm not here about sin, I need direction. I need to talk."

"I'm a priest, not a psychiatrist."

"I know, Father, but—"

"Is that you, Matt Conley?"

He hesitated. "Yes."

The priest sighed. "Meet me out back."

The wooden slider closed. Conley took a deep breath, waited a while after he heard Father McCarrick exit, and opened the door. The priest stood directly in front of him, waiting. Father had lost weight, his cheeks looked taut, and his curly black hair shone. His starched cassock fit him as if tailored.

"About time," he said. "You're not looking so good, Matt."

"Nice to see you too, Father."

The waiting crowd in the last pew turned and watched the interchange. McCarrick saw their stares and told them, "Bio break. Say four or five Hail Marys and I'll credit it toward your penance."

He waved Conley on and they pushed open the big front door. The day was sunshine and warmth.

"Maybe we should talk after you finish confessions, Father."

"Good idea, but a little late, Matt."

He led him to the rectory, a well-kept cottage on the other side of the parking lot. The place was a fraction of the size of Father McCarrick's house at St. Ambrose's. Conley followed and the priest suddenly stopped, turned, and sat on the first step.

Conley sat next to him. "You look good, Father."

"Let's cut the small talk, Matt."

Conley wiped his forehead and drew a breath. "Lisa's failing, Father. I prayed, but nothing worked. I tried love, then discipline. Prayer actually seems to be making things worse."

"Tell me about it. I prayed to save St. Ambrose and

the whole damn church burned down, but He left the people. That was my fault. You see, I should have been more specific."

"But this is much different."

"You don't see me being ungrateful or blaming others. The fact you helped start the fire is not something I dwell on—"

"Father, Simon O'Neil knocked the candles over, candles that wouldn't have been there if you hadn't used the Madonna to fake a miracle—"

"The point, my uncontrite friend, is praying is like drawing a poker hand. Read 'em and weep."

The screen door behind them squealed open, powered by his housekeeper, Mrs. Blodgett. When she smiled, it was something Conley realized he'd never seen. Her hair was cut short, her austere housedress replaced with a smart outfit, and she looked happy and relaxed. A very different woman from the one he remembered. He couldn't stop staring. She spoke.

"I have tea ready, Father McCarrick, and scones."

Father whispered. "Mrs. B and I accepted the change God gave us, Matt," he said as he climbed the stairs to join her. "With acceptance comes peace." She held the door wide for him and he turned in afterthought, smiling like her.

"Some say unanswered prayers are God's greatest gift, Matt. Keep praying, that's my advice. Be it penance or reward, the Good Lord never misdeals."

Chapter Six

On Memorial Day morning, Conley peered through Angelo's spotless windshield at reporters gathered under the portico of City Hospital. The rumor of a mutilation killing had attracted the vultures. Angelo pounded the steering wheel with his palm and somehow the ash on the smoldering cigarette between his fingers never moved.

"Son of a bitch."

"Gerard's not there," Conley said.

Angelo goosed the gas pedal and the sedan surged, tires squealing, and muscled around a curve in the narrow drive.

"I know where he is," Angelo muttered.

Around the brick building, down a wide, steep ramp. Angelo threw the gearshift into *park* and left the car running, its silver grille kissing the *Ambulance Only* sign. The glass doors to the emergency ward parted with a hiss as they approached. Angelo's dark trench coat flared behind him and his cigarette smoke trailed straight back like a jet's contrail. Rows of chairs were arranged in the lobby like theater seats. Bodies—sprawled, pensive, sleeping—occupied most of them.

An anguished scream came from the room on the left. An old man in a khaki uniform shuffled backward out of it into the hall, working a mop whose head was red with blood.

Conley and Angelo marched the well-lighted hallway. Shades of white glimmered around them—on floor, walls, and doorways—from fluorescents that lined the ceiling like bright veins. A silver elevator opened to reveal a young woman, wheelchair-bound, with a baby in her arms. A young man stood next to her, holding a large suitcase that pulled his arm straight. A matron wheeled the chair, hurrying to introduce the infant to the outside world, hardly waiting for Conley and Angelo to step back. The attendant eyed Angelo's cigarette disapprovingly.

Angelo stepped forward when they cleared, and stopped the closing door with the back of his free fist. They descended and the elevator opened to underground dampness. The hall was whiter than the one above. Tiles sparkled. Sweet air descended from ceiling vents.

Angelo pushed the plain wooden door in front of them. A large room was on the other side, bathed in harsh light and still air. Empty silver beds stood in formation. The farthest one wasn't empty. The girl from the rose garden lay on the gurney.

Alice. She had a name now. No longer called victim, female, corpse. *Alice Starke.*

Angelo drew on his cigarette in satisfaction as Gerard stood over her along with three men in scrubs, masked and capped. He turned and marched to Conley and Angelo, hatless, a bent arm trapping his cap against his side.

"Show some respect," he said, lips hardly moving.

"I am," Angelo said, smoke streaming from his nostrils.

"Then step outside."

Behind them the men pulled the sheet down from Alice. They placed a body block under her shoulder blades, and her chest thrust upward. They used long scalpels on her and liquid sluiced slowly through the serrated tray and collected into the solid one beneath. The patter grew. The smell of formaldehyde mixed with fetid stench.

"We want the autopsy report first, before you give it to the state dicks," Angelo said.

"Why?"

"We've got leads, your guys don't."

"What leads?"

"Just trust us, Roland."

"No." Gerard shook his head and tried to walk past.

Angelo locked the inside latch to the morgue door and stood in front of it. Light played off Gerard's bald head. His face was a long slate of resolve.

A saw sprang to life behind them, its shrill sound deepening to a dull scrape. Gerard's face twitched and the lines in it seemed to form into deep, dark cracks.

"You are one special asshole," Gerard hissed at Angelo.

When they'd found her, Alice's body still showed tone and tightness and tan. Her fetal curl said little girl—she'd wake soon, and uncurl, stretch, and yawn. Now she was the color of putty and every inch of her body quivered as they worked on her.

Gerard's cheek pulsed. He was obviously uncomfortable. Silence seeped through the room, until the saw started again.

"All right," he said to Angelo.

"Didn't hear you, Captain."

"I said all right, you fucker. You'll get the report,

but understand this. You work for me now and you damn well better share every bit of evidence you morons stumble upon. Now step out of my way."

Conley flipped the latch and opened the door. They backed into the hallway and Gerard followed, closed the door, and took three quick steps toward Angelo. "Did you hear me?" he snarled.

Angelo dropped the cigarette and crushed it between heel and tile. He reopened the door and cupped a hand to his ear. "What's that, Gerard? All I can hear is the whine of a saw and the snap of breaking bones."

Chapter Seven

On the Tuesday after Alice Starke's murder, Gerard sent Conley to visit her workplace. Picketers walked a lazy circle in front of Gray's Tannery, carrying white placards nailed to poles and two-by-fours. Their owners dug free hands into the pockets of heavy coats.

UNITE, read one sign, and it seemed to be a command for the strikers to close ranks against the cold.

SLAVERY, read another, and the word suited their dress and demeanor—ill-fitting clothes and downturned faces that studied shuffling boots.

They stopped to let Conley through and swarmed back to their round walk when he passed. Two uniformed cops stood near a barrel fire that stunk like wet dog.

Glass doors opened on a lobby with an unattended desk and a cracked leather couch. No pictures on the walls, just a scarred wooden door in the dark paneling. The door opened and the old man stood in the threshold for a moment, as if posing for a full-length portrait. Gray's appearance matched his name—washed-out eyes that swam behind thick glasses, colorless hair—what was left of it—and mottled skin, a patchwork of whiteness and liver spots.

A man followed him—young, with long, dark hair

flowing past his shoulders and a weight lifter's build. Gray introduced him as Patrick Runyan, and he squeezed Conley's hand so hard it forced a quick breath.

"Mr. Runyan's my new security chief," Gray said. "I hired him to protect my loyal workers from the ingrates outside."

"Your name's familiar," Conley said to Runyan. "Where've I heard it?"

"You're confusing me with someone else, Detective. Lots of Runyans on the North Shore these days." They entered the tannery, and the stink of chemicals seemed to give the air weight. Grime caked the floor and a sticky skin of dirt-caked gum oozed when he stepped on it. The concrete walls wore it too, a scum that looked like hair.

They walked a wide aisle, and Runyan slowed and hung behind Gray's shoulder.

"I'm a busy man," Gray said. "The police already asked their questions, Detective."

"You know how questions are," Conley said. "They breed."

Man-high rafters stood to their right and wooden arches of timber rocked leather skins in a shallow trough of foaming liquid. Two men slung leathers over the few remaining bare beams. The bottoms of rough hides slapped the dirty river and the rocking timbers pulsed like heaving ribs.

"Alice Starke used drugs, Detective. Simple as that. Unhappy with this world's reality, she decided to make one of her own."

They passed a large cylinder, a discolored metal drum turning, tumbling, and banging. They climbed wide steps with worn treads, and walked to an area filled with heavy tables surrounded by women in kerchiefs and aprons. They stopped pressing heavy irons on the brown paper that covered leather pieces, and smiled at Gray, their lips closed, their eyes vacant.

"How long did she work for you?" Conley said.

"A year or so. Joined her mother on the line."

"Alice worked with her mother?"

Gray looked at him and his eyes seemed to still, galvanize, and harden.

"Until Sarah Starke passed."

"When? How?"

"Last month. Sarah was driven by diligence and finally consumed by her magnificent work ethic. Doctors said heart attack, but I prefer my version."

Gray waved his hand toward the table.

"She died right here. I held her in my arms and listened to her last breath."

He folded his hands and stood silent, as if expressing tribute to Sarah Starke's honorable death— and sorrow for Alice's dishonorable life. The chant outside suddenly got louder, the voices urgent. A bottle broke. A crash sounded.

Gray looked up as if he'd just detected something in the air. He adjusted his milky glasses and spoke to the space.

"Runyan, entertain the detective."

Gray set off toward the way they'd come and Runyan stepped forward. Conley looked toward the women.

"Did you know Alice?" he said to the group.

Runyan walked to the closest woman and leaned over her shoulder, so close his long hair teased the top of her scoop-neck T-shirt.

"They'll not talk to you, Detective."

"Why?"

"Loyalty? Prudence? Fear? Take your pick." Runyan walked to another, a young lady with red, ruddy cheeks. The women worked silently, expressionless, as if Runyan weren't invading their space. As if Runyan weren't even there. As if Runyan were…

An apparition?

"You knew her, Mr. Runyan?"

"I knew her type, Detective. Mr. Gray and I differ about her failure. Drugs weren't the problem. They were the last link in a very rusted chain."

"What's your theory, Mr. Runyan?"

"A life obsessed with entitlement, much like the miscreants outside. Failures covet the trappings of success. Strength defines goodness, Detective. Sarah was strong. Alice was weak. That's your answer."

The din outside grew louder. Conley headed for a cathedral window at the end of the aisle. Runyan kept with him this time, not off the shoulder. The clang of the tannery's machines became a drumbeat.

They reached the window. The crowd outside had morphed from circle to triangle and the leaders were banging on the door. Speeding cars braked to a stop and burly men piled out. They carried lumber too, but not wood for signs. Clubs, bats, and tire irons.

Strikebreakers.

The picketers shrank against the building. The two cops drifted away from the fire can and walked slowly into the street to keep order.

A standoff. Muffled words and threatening gestures

between policemen and the newcomers. A bat was raised quickly and swung across the lead cop's chest. He went down, twisting, writhing. Both sides seemed to freeze from the suddenness, the unreality.

As if by signal, the groups charged each other, a clatter of footsteps, a chop of sticks. Shouts. Cries. The second cop fell and Conley turned to the stairs.

Runyan stood before him.

"Best you stay, Detective."

Runyan spread his hand, and thick splayed fingers with blunt tips dug into Conley's chest like steel rods.

"Mr. Runyan," Conley said, "now I remember you. You were an enforcer for that Chelsea protection crew that got busted last year. How much is Gray paying you to intimidate the union?"

"I'm a security consultant, Detective. Just like you. Our titles simply depend on who writes our paychecks." He nodded toward the window. "Would you deny the marchers a chance to prove their character?"

Conley tried to move the arm, but its strength was terrible—hard muscle, like smooth rock in a stretched sleeve.

"Move away."

"I can't let you go, Detective. Best you stay, really. Not your fight. Tell your superiors you didn't know, you were unaware."

Runyan cupped his shoulder with an open hand and pushed him away from the window.

"What's it like to be so noble, Detective? To stand up for someone you don't even know? I often wonder."

Conley stepped back, swung his Glock from its holster, and pressed the barrel into the middle of Runyan's forehead. He pressed hard, reddening the skin. Conley's elbow quivered, then he raised it high and tightened his arm.

"You said strength defined goodness. How's this for goodness?" he hissed.

The shouts outside continued. The giant tumbler at the bottom of the stairs banged its cargo. Skins slapped in the chemical trough.

Runyan smiled and moved aside.

Conley raced down the stairs and the clack of his footsteps echoed. He burst through the front door, into the street, gun held high in his trembling hand.

Chapter Eight

A shroud of fog lifted and the sun found the Conleys. Its shine warmed Matt's face and dappled Lisa's hair with highlights as white as milk. Its brightness washed dirt and stains from the cracked concrete of the midway stretched before them.

Two weeks had passed since the discovery of Alice Starke's body, a collection of frustrating 18-hour days with nothing to show. The killer hadn't left a clue, an oddity that puzzled Conley. The autopsy report revealed nothing of value, no DNA. Conley reluctantly decided to take Saturday off, rationalizing Lisa needed some outdoor therapy, but his conscience said the real reason was he needed a break from failure—and Angelo's caustic voice.

A calliope whistled. A roller coaster car climbed its starting track with a crisp ratchet. Barkers called from their booths and pointed to plump stuffed animals on the walls behind them, bowling pins, and plastic ducks in a trough. A group of teenaged girls passed, all giggles and whispered conspiracies, trailing a bouquet of perfume and bubble gum. The Conleys strolled the midway happily, sandals flapping, beach towels tucked under their arms.

Lisa dug her face into his shoulder.

"Cold?" he said.

She looked up and smiled. "Not at all."

He hadn't seen that smile in years. A pleasant sight, even though tiny fans wrinkled the corners of her mouth now.

The walkway was lined with T-shirt shops, souvenirs, and long grills piled with sausage and onions. A man in a leather vest stood sentry in front of a tattoo shop. Flowing script covered his arms. Posters hung in the windows behind him—a dragon with jagged scales and tiny wings curled around a gleaming sword with jewels in handle and hilt—a snake with black triangles on its green back, camouflage skin. A bar on the right—The South Seas. Bamboo stems covered its façade, and black tarpaper showed where pieces had cracked or fallen away. The front door was propped open with a wooden stool, and the inside looked as sunless as a tomb. Glasses clinked, laughter rippled. Silhouettes moved listlessly, and cigarette smoke drifted like a curious mist and hung in the doorway. He pulled her more closely to his side, but Lisa didn't seem affected by the familiar smell of alcohol.

The midway ended at the beach and their feet sank into sand. The sounds of honky-tonk faded. They walked to a quiet place away from the crowd. She laid her towel in the sand, dropped to her knees, and lifted her beach dress. The paleness of her skin was startling against her black swimsuit. Ribs showed, but not like they had during the worst times, when she looked ready to waste away. Today her body looked young and supple again.

They sat, their arms hugging their knees. Two boys flew kites nearby. The taller one's soared, banking and rising. The other boy's suddenly skidded and plowed through sand, and he dragged it ferociously, determined.

"Sweetheart," Lisa called to him. "Your string's tangled. Let me help."

The boy came to her and she cradled the spool on her palm, fingers drumming like delicate pistons on the tangled mess, tapping the twine as if she held some secret knowledge of knots. She pulled the string and it loosened. Loops grew in wide arcs around her straightened hand. Satisfied, she rewrapped the cylinder.

She smiled, eyes squinting, and handed the spool to the boy. He said nothing, but his bright grin was thanks enough. He ran, payed out the line, jerked it quick, and the kite took flight.

Conley watched as she lay on the towel. He rubbed her shoulder and she closed her eyes.

"Let's swim," he said.

"Later."

He shook his head. "C'mon. Later never comes, Lisa."

He helped her up and they crossed hard sand to the waterline. When she was ankle deep, she stopped.

"It's too cold, Matt."

"It's never too cold." He broke into a run and dove into a breaking wave. She stayed, hugging herself.

"You're crazy!" she yelled, and he turned on his back and swam farther out. "You'll turn to ice!" Another yell and a healthy laugh. He watched her return to the blanket and experienced a rush he hadn't felt for ages. She was improving, she was *trusting* him to do the thing he was born to do—to help her.

Cold sea against his back, warm sunshine on his

chest, he turned and dove under. The brisk sting of the water, and maybe the fine day he and his wife were finally having, soothed his gnawing despair over her alcoholism, and helped quiet the voices that had haunted him since he and Angelo found Alice Starke in the woods, voices that were incessant. The frigid water also helped silence Angelo's hateful insults, his dour opinions, his black disposition, his soullessness.

Conley dove again, deeper, to colder water. The icy rush was invigorating. When he surfaced, he saw the kite had risen and fluttered in the wind with seagulls and terns.

A cry came from shore. The boy was knee-deep in the surf and the spool in his hand was empty. The end of the string skimmed the waves.

Conley kicked hard and swam to the moving string. A wave slowed him, but then he dug his hands harder, carving the water, kicking as hard as he could. Almost there. Nothing was as important as the challenge of rescuing the kite. His hand reached out and grasped it, a slippery tickle on his palm. He looked up. The kite hung still, as if waiting. Suddenly another wave lifted him and the string slid through his hand as if greased.

The kite rose on a gust that seemed to match the rolling wave. He swam again, farther out. The string simply skipped now, just touching the water. Finally it lifted with a snap and spray, and flew.

He treaded water and caught his breath. The boy was gone, and his empty plastic spool bounced in the surf.

Lisa's towel lay bare, an edge folded over, sand blowing across it.

He swam toward shore, breathless, fighting the

riptide, and he called her name against the roaring surf. He ran past the towel and stepped onto the rough surface of the midway, sandpaper on his bare feet.

Maybe she went for a walk. Maybe she was looking for him. Maybe.

The calliope shrilled. An empty car hurtled along the coaster tracks like a runaway train. The tattooed sentry in front of the store was gone. Laughter spilled from The South Seas. Conley stepped inside, let his eyes adjust to the dark, and headed toward the crowd at the bar. The red-faced patrons turned to him and laughed harder. Their circle parted.

Lisa sat on a man's lap, his grubby hands kneading her hips. Her top was off, her white skin exposed. She drank a clear liquid, hands tight around the glass as if it were a precious thing. When she saw him she drank faster.

He pushed the laughing patrons aside, and when he seized her wrist and pulled her off the man's lap the glass fell and smashed on the floor. The laughter stopped, voices roared, and the bartender clapped his hand on the bar for order.

Shards of glass cut into Conley's bare feet. Lisa lunged away, sluicing her hand through a puddle on the bar, and licking her fingers like a child. The crowd roared again—not words this time, just sounds. He elbowed the blackshapes away as they pawed at the two of them like hungry Morlocks. Her bikini top was nowhere in sight. He grabbed a damp bar towel with one hand to cover her and dragged her toward the lighted doorway with the other. Blood rushed in his ears. When it subsided, the old voices returned.

Kill them! Angelo screamed. *Kill the*

motherfuckers. Every one!

Glass dug deeper into his feet with every step, and he slid on his blood.

Strength is goodness, Runyan hissed, and Conley felt strong fingers prod his chest three times, a beat for every word.

Lisa fought to stay, clawing at tables and chairs for anchor, and the scrape of wooden legs across the floor sounded like the unnerving whir of the surgical saw the doctors used on the corpse of Alice Starke.

He kept on.

To the light.

Through the swirling smoke.

Onto the midway.

Chapter Nine

Captain Roland Gerard knelt on a purple kneeler on the last week of June. His aching knees sank into the plush leather and knocked against the padded wood. His elbows settled on an armrest and he peered into the casket.

He'd attended the police academy with Tim Miller, and remembered he looked young enough to be a high schooler. The corpse in front of him looked artificial, a wax replica. Lips had disappeared, replaced with two thin red lines. Cheeks looked like pancakes dusted with flour. A silver shock of hair was the only authentic part of the man, a lock of it spilling over his forehead like an errant comma. A sea of flowers hung overhead, a sweet-smelling wave flowing over an army of pedestals. Silk ribbons hung from the center of bouquets like golden tongues. *DAD*, said one, *GRAMPA*, wagged another.

"Everything all right?"—a whisper in his ear, a raspy coo.

He turned.

Julius Silsbee, funeral director, was at his shoulder, wearing a crisp black suit, his words flavored with spearmint breath savers. A line of old women stood behind him, frowning at Gerard.

"Many are waiting," Silsbee said.

Gerard rose and pushed Silsbee's helping hand

away. His legs were numb, knees shaky, so he slapped his palms on the front of his pants as if to smooth them.

Mrs. Miller sat just beyond the casket, eyes puffy, her lace handkerchief balled in her hand.

"Trudy," he said, "I'm so sorry."

"I know you are, Roland. Tim's big heart finally gave out. It was so sudden."

She took his hand and the damp handkerchief fell across his wrist.

"You and Tim were such good friends. Like brothers."

He squeezed her hands.

"He looks good, Trudy. Must have been a content man when God called him."

"You and Tim were so alike. Same careers, same lives."

Alike? Not quite. Truth was, Tim was old before his time. A drinker and a womanizer—did Trudy know? Either way, Tim had chosen the undisciplined life that led to his death. He was a good bad example—that was his legacy. Gerard refused to make that mistake. There was a lot more life left in Roland Gerard. He kept his mind young and his body trained.

He turned. "Good crowd for your Tim. You should be proud."

A long silence followed, and he tried to leave, but she didn't let go. The wet handkerchief seemed to be stiffening on his wrist, binding his hand, and he tried to work it away. Her strength was incredible, the clamping of her hand, the steel bands of her fingers. He pulled hard, twice, three times. Her fingers opened and the handkerchief floated to his feet.

An old woman in a flower print dress stepped

toward her, but Silsbee was quicker. He genuflected and scooped the hanky in one motion.

Trudy's eyes were wide now and her fingers resembled pale, frozen talons. She shrank from Gerard.

He turned his palm sideways, patted her shoulder and smiled.

"See you at the funeral in the morning, dear."

He made his way from parlor to hallway, a long gallery hung with portraits of dead Silsbees. The last one he encountered was alive—the doorman, a young apprentice who opened the door and wished him good night.

****

The next morning, the sound of bagpipes rolled across the cemetery as somber policemen marched behind Tim Miller's gold coffin. Gerard followed in the rear, and when he stopped he folded his hands and rested them on his belt buckle. The crowd stared in the general direction of Trudy and her family. The priest finally spoke.

"Welcome the Lord into your life every day…"

When he was finally done, two of Tim's brood climbed the green skirt surrounding the grave and threw carnations into the open hole. Hundreds of mourners stood motionless until the priest walked away. The District Attorney was suddenly beside Gerard.

"Are you close to finding Alice Starke's killer?"

Young, impatient, inexperienced. A bureaucrat, a climber, that's what he was. Elected DA was first rung on the ladder to political greatness—an oxymoron if ever there was one.

"We're still working—"

"Answer the question."

"Nothing yet," Gerard said. "It takes time."

"You've had a month and word is you've got nothing." The DA's jaw twitched. "Did I make a mistake choosing you, Gerard? Chief Detective Kerrigan told me Detective Angelo has a name."

Gerard placed his cap on his head, turned from the DA, and attacked the hill. After an hour of eulogies and prayers, and a stinging lecture from his young superior, Gerard carried only two words away from the graveside ceremony.

Detective Angelo.

****

Tick—and echo. Water dripped. A floor buffer whirred somewhere in the building. Half the overhead fluorescents were off and the empty squad room was filled with shadows. The DA's challenge still rang in Gerard's ears as he walked between crowded desks. Chairs were tucked underneath, all except Angelo's. His was two feet away from his desk, as if the asshole's ghost were sitting in it.

His in-basket was full of papers and folders. Gerard lifted the pile and buried the sealed, blank envelope containing Alice Starke's autopsy report.

Fuck Angelo. Let him find it.

He stood in front of the desk and imagined he was Angelo, ready to sit. He imagined opening the brown folder that sat in the middle of the blotter.

The swoosh of the buffer got louder, closer.

He sat. The corner of the folder was raised in invitation.

Tick.

Whir.

He fit the tip of his finger under the folder flap.

A photograph sat on top—black and white, but those seemed to be the only colors the subject needed. Dark eyes, dark hair, dark skin. He had a wisp of a goatee, long hairs cropped and pointing down like an arrowhead.

He pushed the picture aside with the same fingertip, eyes straining in the half-light, and read the page underneath. Words were underlined in red.

Luca Starbird. Profession?—performer.

Aren't we all?

He read the pages under the photo, traffic and vagrancy citations, mostly in seaside cities—Miami, Myrtle Beach, Atlantic City—and a half dozen more. Itinerant. Romany.

Gypsy.

Arrest warrants—bunko, assault, stalking, possession of an illegal knife.

KILLER? Written in what had to be Angelo's bold scrawl.

Gerard closed the folder and stood. He breathed a lungful of air that stunk from an ashtray full of Angelo's cigarette butts—and he left the silent squad room quickly, like a man with new life.

Chapter Ten

"Love and money," Aunt Mara said to Gina on her sixteenth birthday. Remember, that's what the *gadjos* want, what everybody wants. It's always love and money."

Auntie Mara shuffled tarot cards. She trained her brown eyes on Gina, selected a card without looking, and raised it in front of her round face so it kissed her cracked lips. The card was busy and colorful—Adam and Eve standing naked under an open-winged angel.

"Lovers," she said and laid it on the table between them.

More shuffling—slow, then fast. This time Auntie raised a picture of a numbered wheel in front of her crooked nose. Gina smiled because Mara looked like she had three eyes.

"Fortune."

"You couldn't see," Gina said. "How did you know?"

Mara's eyes narrowed as she turned the card and whispered.

"Look closely, Gina."

Her aunt touched the yellow, crusted stain on the back of the fortune-eye card. Next she turned the tarot of the shameless lovers and tapped a fingertip on the delaminated corner.

Mara grinned and chortled. Spittle formed on her

chin. "Gypsy magic," she said with a wide smile, and spread her chubby fingers across the deck. "This is your gift, Gina. Practice and you'll be a seer just like your aunt."

****

Luca dug in front of the tent and plunged the end of a two-by-four into the hole. He stood on a crate and drove the wood deep with a hammer, muscled arms flexing. Finally the wood didn't move, but vibrated like a musical instrument. Pura handed him a nail, and he pounded it into the top and hung a sign—FORTUNES. Streamers were added, colorful ribbons fluttering from the rusty stud.

Gina folded her arms and turned away. Pura's shuffling feet hissed through the grass behind her. The toolbox clapped shut. She knew from the gentle clank of tools Luca had lifted the box and was carrying it, walking close to their grandfather, as always, ready to catch him if his old legs stumbled.

Best not to listen to the sounds she knew so well, or to watch her grandfather and brother leave. Better to look at the majestic green mountains surrounding this hidden field, or at the silent house at its edge. She imagined repairing its tarpaper walls and broken stairs, and living in such a home instead of campers and tents.

Squeak and slam. Sounds carried from the nearby silver trailer, a bawdy house with neon lights. Its swinging, pink-tasseled door worked hard, waving a parade of bikers and mountain men inside. A black woman barked from the steps like a carnival hawker, calling men to sin.

Gina swore she would always remember this Ozark hell as the place where her grandfather and aunts betrayed her. The aunts had turned her into a fake psychic and Pura taught Luca to stage dogfights for money. The sight of her brother carrying bleeding strays to chicken-wire pens made her cry, and seeing him carry still canvas sacks to the river at midnight made her want to die. But Pura ignored her pleas, and had become strangely silent.

She leaned against the pole in front of her tent. The band was setting up on a stage in the field, and the singer waved to her. Lately she'd begun to think of him and her as *us*, even though a few kisses, caresses, and sweet words behind the bandstand were all they'd shared. Pura and her aunts would disapprove if they knew, and that seemed to make it more delicious. *Gadjo*, they'd tell her in disgust. *Outsider*.

If outsiders were kind to dogs and looked down on cheating the desperate and lonely with marked cards, maybe they weren't so evil. The band uncased their instruments. The singer pushed back his long hair, curled it over an ear, and smiled at her.

They tuned up, and sour notes and staccato runs cut the thin mountain air. Her long-haired boy cradled the microphone, and the musicians began a better melody—drums first, guitar, a fiddle—and beautiful music filled a place that needed it badly.

The overpowering fragrance of sharp perfume enveloped her. The pink-trailer madam stood on the other side of the board, streamers collected in her dark fist. Her breasts heaved under a low-cut dress, necklace and bracelet sparkled in the stingy sun, and blue shoes shined—except where orange mud from the dirt trails had caked.

"Mmmm-mmm, you is a package. You be the rose

in this here thorn patch, honey."

Gina opened the flap to the tent. Lit candles made the inside glow like a royal court. She swept her free arm toward the entrance, just like her aunts had taught her to.

"I know your future."

The madam walked in and smiled. "I know my future too, Gypsy girl. Same as the present and just like the past. Sure as arithmetic."

Gina sat, arms extended, palms flat on the table. "The tarot," she explained in the deep voice Mara had instructed her to use.

"Yessirree, I know the tay-roh, sweetie. My Louisiana granny worked that ju-ju."

Madam handed her five dollars. Gina felt the crispness of the new bill, the coldness. She placed it deep in her dress pocket and had the madam cut the deck. Gina shuffled the cards and cocked her head when her lover started to sing. His voice was her favorite instrument. A card missed her hand and fell to the ground, and when she reached for it her chair almost overturned. Madam seized her wrist.

"How long you been doin' this, girl?"

Gina sat straight in her chair and looked away. A song verse started and finished. Madam let go.

"This ain't you, sweetie. The Good Lord gives everyone a gift, but this ain't yours."

Gina shuffled again, harder. The bass pounded a second heartbeat in her chest. The fiddle strummed a long note. Her *gadjo* sang.

"No pleasure here on earth I find…"

"Here, girl, you listen to me," Madam said. "You got the gifts every woman is born with, and they'll get you through your life jus' fine. You come work with us and your future will be better than Gypsy magic, guaranteed."

More words from the sad, beautiful song outside. *"Love—I've seen trouble all my days…"*

"This world takes us all down, sweetie, every one of us," Madam said. "Fill your pockets with cash. Makes the fall softer."

Gina felt the cards and searched for the one with the crusted stain. She found the Wheel of Fortune, but when she slapped the card in front of her, it slid off the table onto the ground. She closed her eyes. Madam stood.

"Growin' up's the hardest work, little girl. You think on what I said and when you arrive at the right answer, come see me. Our little family will be waitin'."

Madam left and the tent flap settled behind her. Gina knelt on the ground and searched for the lost card. She crawled under the table in her long dress, gathering it so she could move easier, and experienced a depression as dark as her lover's song.

Madam was right. Cheating with cards was no gift, and Pura and her aunts—her family, her *kumpania*—no longer seemed a blessing. Lying to the desperate and lonely with the tarot was as bad as whoring in the silver-pink trailer. As bad as sacrificing dogs for sport, making money from the blood of animals whose fatal mistake was trusting man.

Love was the answer, but not the kind you sold. Did her long-haired boy love her? She'd find out. Did he love her enough to take her from this place? She'd find that out too.

She stood, pressing the card against her chest, and

caught a breath. A mountain man sat in the chair on the other side of the table, a thin hayseed with a straw hat, and a wrinkled face with beard stubble and a deep dimple.

"Says *Fortunes* outside," he said, stroking his chin with a weathered hand. "I need you to tell mine."

The candles flickered in the waning daylight. She dropped the cards on the table, sat, and collected them. His eyes swiveled to watch her shuffle. The brim of his hat drew a shadow on his face, a craggy map of acne and scars. The long sleeves of a white linen shirt weren't long enough to cover his arms, and the way he held them straight, the way they flared to his wide hands, made them look like broadswords. When he nodded, his rank body odor scented the air.

He held out his hand and dropped three crumpled bills in her palm, and when his long fingers touched hers, a sudden energy surged through them. She sat back, stunned, and caught her breath. She had him cut the deck, and the next time she handled the cards, they felt different. She was suddenly dizzy, overcome by vertigo. The walls of the tent pulsed, even though the air outside was still. She looked down and was surprised to see her hands working fast. Her head began to ache, a stinging pick at both temples. The cards shuffled with a shooshing sound. She dealt. He leaned forward and his hot breath washed her face. She threw a card and it landed on the table with a snap—the warrior on his horse.

He grunted.

More cards, and to her surprise they angled perfectly from center to left, alternate corners touching. He stared at her eyes, and his gaze seemed to bore through her skull. The temple pain traveled to the center of her head and became a vision, a movie as clear as the lighted frames in Pura's old stereoscope—the mountain man standing on a riverbank and watching a still body turn a cartwheel in black water.

Slap. First card on the right side, another perfect angle, the beginning of a triangle. The tarot showed a medieval man in a boat, pushing a long punt with a pole.

The hayseed slid his hand over his mouth.

More pain, another vision—wet dirt, a mud-caked shovel, a dainty piece of fabric half-buried in freshly-dug soil. The hayseed leaned on the shovel and wiped his brow.

Card slap. The wheel.

Her hands built the rest of the flat card pyramid. Outside, the bass thundered and the fiddle screamed.

Final cards. She turned one like a spindle and watched herself place it dead center in the triangle. The Lovers. Another tarot, the last—a hanging man.

He leaned across the table, clutched her blouse, and bunched it in his hand.

"The way I read it," he said, dark eyes burning, his voice rasping, "you and me's meant for each other."

The other hand curled into a fist—raw-boned and white-knuckled. The object hidden in his hand shone, his thumb moved, and a knife blade sprung from the fist. He raised the knife overhead, plunged it through the back of the tent, and cut a flap from top to bottom. He stepped through and dragged her into the field. Dusk was setting in, the sun dropping behind the green mountain. Unmuffled by the tent, the music was clearer. Her *gadjo* swayed on the stage, and she called to him as loudly as she could. The singer turned slightly, pale blue eyes shining through his beautiful curls. Then a chord changed and he focused back on the crowd and sang.

Mountain man toiled steadily across the field. He started to whistle, and she realized it was just the exhalation of his laboring breath. She fought, but that terrible grip never tired, and they trudged toward the house, a foreboding structure now that looked like it could never be anyone's home. Through the front door, into a room with peeling paint and trash strewn on the wide-plank floor, along with needles and syringes, and a solitary worn couch. Two people lay there, pale and still as cadavers, studying the ceiling with vacant stares.

She stumbled again and was pulled through a door into a dark room, onto a moist, musty mattress. Mountain man knelt over her and removed the shirt from his hairy torso. When he climbed on her his weight made it hard to breathe. He pressed the flat of his blade against her cheek, tore her blouse, and kissed her. His scaly arms scraped like sandpaper. His tongue crept from his mouth and the slimy fat worm traveled her cheek, eyelids, ears. The knife point hurt like a burning coal.

Suddenly different flesh shot across his chest from behind—a smooth arm, not like the rugged hayseed's, but muscled and hairless, curling around his neck like a snake. His stone eyes opened wide and he tried to get free, struggling and bucking like a fighting fish. She was pummeled by knees, hips, and elbows as he fought, until she heard his breath weaken and finally stop. She pushed him onto the floor, and her monstrous visions of him suddenly disappeared. This man would rape and kill no more.

Luca crouched over her, closed her blouse, and lifted her in his arms easily, as if she were a child. He nuzzled her cheek with his peach fuzz.

"Gina," he said, and the word was great comfort. She'd begun to fear this new power she possessed—a power that allowed her to see the past of others like newsreels and deal their future with lightning hands, with hands that seemed to belong to someone else.

"Come," he whispered. "Pura says it's time to leave."

Chapter Eleven

Random Independence Day fireworks flared overhead in the fading light of dusk. Conley picked up a spear, a two-by four whose end had been burned to a point. Black bubbles lined the spearhead, charred wood that shone like polished stones in the light of a Roman candle. He and Angelo forged ahead and crossed a meadow in Ocean Park Woods, not far from where they'd found the body of Alice Starke.

Angelo's car sat behind them, engine cooling and pinging like a slow-tolling bell. They approached a gully with thick, furry grass on the sides. Homeless people reclined on blankets or slept inside the gully, limbs akimbo, strewn like casualties on a battlefield. The coming of summer had swelled their numbers.

Conley shuffled sideways down a wall, the bottom of his foot still tender where the glass had cut him in The South Seas. Angelo stood at the top of the berm, legs spread, thumbs hooked into his belt on either side of a glistening buckle, head bent toward his partner.

"Make it quick," he shouted. Angelo made no bones about this assignment from Gerard. Checking out the homeless camp was a useless exercise, beneath his duty, and furthermore he had his own leads to follow. Besides, if a lead of Gerard's provided a clue, that was worse than failure, it was humiliation.

Earthy smells, the stink of urine, feces, and body

odor hung in the ditch, a fragrant cloud trapped in the green womb. Wet cardboard partially covered a sleeping figure. Conley fit the spear point under the cover and lifted. It separated into dark, corrugated layers and broke in frayed pieces, shedding slowly, as if reluctant to reveal what was underneath. He removed layer after layer until the sleeping bum was uncovered.

A monochrome man—with gray hair, drab clothes, slate-colored skin, mumbled. He slept like a child, his hairy head on folded hands. Conley crouched and held the man's chin between thumb and forefinger.

"Did he say good morning or good night?" Angelo sneered.

Conley ignored the sarcasm and continued in Angelo's shadow to the next sleepers, past empty wine bottles, plastic bags, and Styrofoam containers. Two pairs of arms poked out from under a dirty blanket, with blackened fingernails and skin so brown it looked like leather.

Farther down the gully a dog lifted its head, sprang to life, and charged Conley, barking and snarling. The mongrel's hair was matted, except for a tuft rising from its neck like a mane. When Conley ignored him and lifted the next blanket, the dog quieted and joined him over the pair. The mutt's tail began to wag as he sniffed them energetically.

A man and a woman lay together. Their faces looked like red masks, hers a puzzle of scars, his a map of rosacea bisected by a bulbous nose.

"Three curs," Angelo said from above and bared his teeth in a smile.

Rustling sounded ahead, and a man jumped to his feet and sprinted up the side of the ditch. He was younger than the rest, and from his fearful expression, Conley saw he was unlike the others in another way. He *had* knowledge.

Conley dropped the wood and climbed the hill. Angelo was already chasing the runner, and when Conley finally reached the top of the rise, he saw nothing but the wide skirts of fir trees at the edge of the forest. He slid back into the gully where the man had been and found a black cloth on the grass. He retrieved a pencil from his jacket, slid the blunt end under, and raised it to eye level. A dress, short and sheer. Red panties lay underneath, caked with dirt.

Angelo returned, panting.

"Lost the fucker," he said. "Let's get out of here."

"We need to find him. This might be Alice's."

Conley lifted the clothes and the dainty things swayed on the pencil.

Angelo shook his head. "That's nothing," he said. "Nothing. Dude could be a cross dresser…or a pervert. He probably stole 'em off a clothesline."

The dog approached Angelo, snarling and snapping.

"Waste of time," Angelo said. "I found the Gypsies. That scum-sucking knife thrower is Alice Starke's killer. I'm sure of it. We'll run his ass in soon."

Angelo spat and the dog jumped away. It suddenly charged and bit Angelo's ankle, tearing his pant leg. Angelo kicked the mutt away, drew his Beretta, and shot it in the back. The dog yipped and collapsed, its matted fur wet with blood, and an anguished cry rose from a bum at the end of the gully.

"Jesus, Angelo!" Conley shouted.

"Happy, Conley?" Angelo wore a smirk, an

unusual expression given the circumstances. He pointed the gun at the dog as if planning to shoot the still body. "That was your fault. I'm out of here, we've wasted enough time."

****

Arthur Starke slouched. The blue vinyl of the padded bench under him crackled, fissures opening wide. The black dress lay on the linoleum table in front of him in a clear plastic bag.

"I don't know, sir," Starke said to Conley. "Oh, Lord, I don't know if it's my Alice's."

Angelo continued to dismiss the importance of the dress Conley had found earlier that evening—no surprise there, his obsession with Luca Starbird left no room for minor concerns such as evidence—and had refused to come. Conley tracked down the homeless man, a vagrant who was in county jail the night Alice was murdered. But Conley felt certain an out-of-place piece of clothing found yards from a murder scene warranted a visit to Alice's father's home, a place she sometimes crashed.

Outside, the steady whoosh of I-95 traffic sounded like a wind tunnel. What kind of childhood did Alice Starke have growing up in this foul, broken-down trailer in a crowded Peabody trailer park? Arthur Starke lifted a can of beer to his lips as if to answer Conley's thought. A drop of condensation splattered on the plastic bag. Starke drank deeply before he spoke.

"My little girl ain't lived here in forever. Tell him, Flo," he said to the woman next to him.

Flo's knitting needles clicked smartly. She was knitting a red square, the white sticks lifting the long stretch of yarn that rose from a basket on the floor. She leaned from her wooden chair and her black hair fell forward to frame her face. She inspected the dress and her caterpillar eyebrows rose. Finally she sat back and the needles resumed their click.

"We caught a homeless person with it. He found it near the glen where we discovered Alice, and was going to give it to his girlfriend. Coroner says it's Alice's size," Conley said. "We'll do a DNA test, but I wanted to show you first."

Starke shook his head and his cheeks puffed. A burp escaped. He squeezed the bridge of his nose, hitched his breath, and closed his eyes.

When he opened them they were even more watery, staring at brown-spotted ceiling tiles. He took another hit of beer.

"Arrest me if you want, but I don't remember, Officer. I don't remember. Alice was just a little girl when my bitch-wife took her away from here."

Gulp. Slurp.

"Can I see her room?" Conley asked.

Starke raised the can higher and shook the last few drops onto his tongue. He suddenly began to cry high-pitched sobs.

Daughter's dead. Beer's gone.

Flo bent sideways, set the needles and square into the basket, and rose. Her white fishnet sweater churned back and forth over her housedress like a sieve. She stood ponderously, but didn't have to take even a step in the tiny trailer to open the refrigerator.

She snapped the pop-top of a fresh beer with a thick finger and stuck her other hand under the hanging flesh of Starke's arm. She lifted him effortlessly, guiding him to a seat only a few feet away, and handed him the can. She snapped the TV on with the remote and voices droned. Leaning over the table, her hand mashing the black dress, she spoke and her breath smelled like sour apples.

"Follow me, Mr. Conley."

She set off down the narrow hallway, hips swaying, floor creaking, and he followed. She opened a door to a tiny room with a bed covered with a faded, salmon-colored spread. Dolls sat on a dresser—arms broken, legs missing, black orbs where eyes had been. Furry little animal pictures lined the walls. A small, mirrored ball hung from a string in the corner.

"That's her dress," Flo said. "This was her room before she left."

Conley opened dresser drawers, most empty, some with faded little-girl clothes. The nightstand drawer contained crayons and lipstick tubes that rolled from back to front.

"You sure?"

"'Course I am. Little tramp stood right here the night she was murdered, titties heavin' in that little thing. I own potholders larger than that dress."

"Arthur wasn't so certain."

"Be serious. Arthur doesn't know when his teeth are in or his dick is out. She was here looking for cash."

"For what?"

She made eye contact and paused to make sure he was listening.

"Scrape job."

Flo walked to the opposite wall and stood next to the louvered windows, bands of light falling on her. "She was gonna stop by the clinic to get an abortion and then probably troll for some stud to knock her up again. Wasn't the first time. That's how Alice rolled, the little slut."

The TV got louder. Arthur hacked, coughed, and gurgled a wet laugh.

"The autopsy report said Alice had needle marks and toxicology found opioids in her system," Conley said.

"No shit, all funded by the Bank of Arthur. She always came here for money," Flo said. "First she sold all the stuff she owned as a kid. Then she got braver. Microwave went missing, and my pearl earrings. After she hawked everything that wasn't nailed down, she badgered Arthur for cash. Swindled him out of most of his pension check some months."

Conley accidentally bumped the hanging ball and it turned, casting tiny squares of light around the room, prism blues, greens, and reds that played across Flo's serious face and sparkled in her glasses like pixie dust.

"Alice leave anything?" she asked. "Rent deposit, insurance?"

"I don't know."

"Well if she did, remember this." Her index finger pointed at the ceiling. "Any money you cops find goes to Arthur C. Starke. The C's for Croyden, by the way."

He grasped the doorknob. She kept on.

"World's a rough place, I tell Arthur." The light show slowed as the ball twisted to a stop. The spin reversed and squares rushed across Flo's face the other way.

"Man's gotta use everything his mama gave him to survive. I tell Arthur to say Croyden nice and loud when he gives his name. Bold and sassy. People always respect a man who's got himself three names."

Chapter Twelve

Brick giants loomed in downtown Ocean Park, tall factories and warehouses checkered with dark windows fortified with steel bars. The buildings cast cold shadows on a vacant lot of broken concrete and asphalt patches, littered with blackened bottle rockets and exploded firecrackers. Open pipes pocked the lot, rusted plumbing that had been cut at ground level. Newspaper and plastic bags blew across the man-made desert like tumbleweeds.

The Gypsy vehicles were parked in circles that carved the space into busy sections. Children swarmed after a ball inside one. Black barrels lay in another, great steel bellies that had been cut in half, filled with burning coals, and laid on metal cross braces. Women grilled meat over them, their faces shiny with perspiration.

On the fifth of July, a dark, depressing day that felt like a holiday hangover, Conley walked between two trucks, scraped his knee on a ball hitch, and headed toward the rumble of voices. A dirt clearing lay in the rear of the lot, surrounded by a circle of chicken wire supported by long stakes. Men stood on the outside, drinking from plastic cups, and smoking cigarettes and cigars. The pungent burn of marijuana tinged the air.

Two boys stood inside the pen, cradling and stroking roosters as if they were infants. Red wattles and crests quivered on the birds' preening heads. One rooster was brown, its feathers rippling shades of auburn as rich as wheat stalks. The other bird was white, with fat, pillowy folds on its chest.

The old Gypsy—Pura—shuffled against the inside of the fence. The knife-thrower—Luca—was close behind. Pura wrote in a notebook and fit a stub of a pencil behind his ear every time he offered his palm, and the dollars he was handed disappeared inside his baggy coat.

The old man finally finished, pockets bulging, pencil parked. He and Luca stepped behind the fence. Conley lowered his ball cap and snapped his coat collar up. Angelo was preparing an arrest warrant for Luca, but Conley was unconvinced of his guilt, so he'd decided to observe and question the Gypsies.

Or was it an excuse to see the Gypsy girl again?

Stillness followed and voices murmured. The boys circled, still petting the birds, and suddenly extended their arms. The birds squawked and their long necks reached toward each other. The boys pulled them back.

Conley edged closer to the pit, past curses, elbows, and the odors of sweat and stale liquor.

The birds reached toward each other again anxiously. This time when the handlers pulled them back they were even more agitated, necks straining, eyes wild.

The crowd surged forward.

The brown bird's feathers rippled its brilliant shades and the white one's roiled like sea foam. The boys couldn't hold them any longer, so they stripped leather sheaths from the birds' legs and three-inch metal spurs gleamed. They heaved them together.

The sidelines erupted, the crowd roared. Fists pumped. The men were as frenzied as the fighters.

Wings fluttered, a blinding flash, a blur. Beaks pecked. Talons raked. The brown bird jumped, steel-first, onto its enemy, and in seconds the white bird's feathers were laced with blood. The brown one was wet too, and when it struck again, hammering its beak into the once-white wing, blood blackened the dirt.

Pura reached his crooked fingers toward the pit, his hands waving in slow, languorous pulls, as if orchestrating the fight. Luca watched quietly. The crowd surged, pressing against Conley's ribs. The roar of the men seemed to excite the birds, lifting the brown one higher. When it came down again, it raked the wounded wing the other way. The white bird's broken wing flailed and it ran in a blood-soaked circle until it finally lay still.

Conley tucked his chin into his chest as Luca opened the gate, lifted the white bird by the neck, and walked by. The boy in the pit gathered the winner in his arms.

Pura stepped into the circle, cash piled on his notepad, and dealt the bills to the small group around him. Luca returned with the rooster, its plucked body pink, raw, and steaming. He handed it to the winner and the boy carried his wounded bird in one arm and the dead one in the other.

Conley was leaving when he saw Pura suddenly turn, the short brim of his porkpie hat lifting slowly, and his dark eyes following him like slow bullets.

Chapter Thirteen

Shoes and boots shuffled and clattered, kicking shards of crumbling white concrete. Men left the cockfight, jostling, laughing, and Conley followed past the sweet smoke of the cooking grills. He was almost to the street when streetlamps clicked on. He passed a beige tent lit by flickering candles inside. A flap covered the front, a purple rectangle decorated with white quarter moons and shooting stars.

The flap opened and Gina's face appeared against the celestial painting. She beckoned to the next woman in line, and the girl followed her inside. Without thinking twice, he queued behind a woman holding an infant.

The wind picked up, sweeping through the lot, and the woman cradled the baby closer. The cool night air amplified its coos and cries.

The girl emerged and hurried away. Gina beckoned mother and child.

A sudden *thwack* sounded from behind. Luca had placed a wood panel in the cockfighting ring, and a crowd had gathered to watch him throw. A rough outline of a man was painted on the board in bright, white paint—outstretched arms, rounded head, and parted legs. Luca threw again and the knife stuck into the center of the head as its handle quivered. Another— in the chest this time. The crowd cheered. The third strike dug into the middle of the groin, and the crowd laughed when he took a mock bow.

A young couple, all giggles and whispers, stepped into line behind Conley. The woman with the baby finally left the tent, head down, arm shielding her face. Gina beckoned him and disappeared into the tent. He pushed the purple curtain aside. The room glowed like a chapel from votive candles that lined the ground around the tent walls. A fat candle in a metal cage swung from the middle of the roof.

She sat in a folding chair behind a round table draped in black cloth, head bowed, long hair flowing over her shoulders. Beads hung around her neck, framed by the open lapels of a silky green blouse. Three decks of cards lay on the table. Throw rugs covered the ground—shags, remnant, Orientals, all torn and tattered.

He sat in the chair facing her and couldn't look away from the face he knew so well—*Lisa's face*. He opened his jacket, unfolded the rap sheet in his pocket, and threw it on the table. He tapped Luca's mug shot hard with the tip of his finger.

"I lied for him," he said. "Did I lie for a killer?"

Outside, the sound of Luca's knife hammered like gunshots. The wind was picking up, filling the tent. The sides stretched toward the candles, billowing and snapping.

"He's done nothing," she said.

He slapped the sheet. "Everyone says he has."

"Don't you see? They say it too many times."

The holder above them swayed and shadows played across the tent's walls, ceilings, carpets.

"Nothing," she repeated. "Nothing."

"Then he'll have nothing to fear when we come for him." *Thwack.*

She covered one of the decks with her hand and slid it into a bag. The second deck followed. She drew the drawstring and left the scattered cards on the table. Fantastical creatures decorated the leftover cards—an angel, a winged lion, a wizard, all with words written underneath.

Temperance
Strength
Magician

The wind suddenly buffeted the tent. Gina rushed to secure the wavering poles on either side of the doorway, and hurried outside to tighten the staked ropes. The far wall fluttered and knocked a candle over, and its flame flickered before liquid wax extinguished it. A second candle fell, rolled, and ignited the Oriental rug's tassels. Fire raced along the edge like a fuse.

The tent wall snapped louder, closer. The wind was working ropes and stakes out of the ground and loosening the flap. The burning rug's tassels twisted and writhed like living things. Another carpet caught fire, a beige oblong remnant shaped like a puzzle piece. Conley jumped up and flipped the rug, stomping its bottom, and heat scorched the soles of his shoes. The hanging candle swung back and forth over an empty chair.

The wind died. Knives no longer barked. Silence filled the tent.

He headed for the purple sheet and it suddenly opened. He looked outside. Luca's board was gone and the fighting ring was empty. Gina, cheeks rosy, eyes glassy, stood in the doorway.

"Where is he?" Conley said. "Where did he go?" She placed her hands on his chest when he tried to leave. He pushed her hands away, but she laced their fingers together. He ached at the feel of her. Her beauty was breathtaking, her touch so divine it made his skin warm.

She's not Lisa.

But she is.

"Sit," Gina urged, "and I'll tell you what you need to know."

He hesitated.

"Sit," she said. "Or you'll never find him."

Conley released the curtain and returned to the table.

"Tell me where he went."

She motioned to the chair and collected the loose cards. "I have a question, Detective. Consider it a trade. Why did you protect Luca at the campground?"

He exhaled and zippered his jacket. "I'll look for him myself."

"You'll be passing on two opportunities. I'll tell you where Luca is and I'll tell you something about yourself. Maybe something you need to know." She shuffled the cards and closed her eyes. "What do you need, Detective? Think. What do you need the most?"

Lisa—

She opened her eyes slowly. "You're thinking of your woman. All right. The tarot will tell us about her."

She turned three cards.

"You've known each other a long time. You were young together. You want to grow old with her."

I do.

She touched the cards tentatively and dealt three

77

more. Suddenly she winced and pressed her throat. "So much pain," she said. "So much."

"Where's Luca?" he said, his mouth dry.

"Too much pain to bear. A child has died."

The overhead light rocked slowly, like a pendulum. He stared at the cards, not seeing any of them.

Brendan.

She dealt another card to his left, swords sunk at angles into a mound—*Ten of Swords.*

"More pain," she said. "But peace follows."

Matt couldn't imagine how. First Brendan, now Lisa.

She dropped the middle card, a long-legged man dressed as a jester, stepping toward the edge of a cliff—*The Fool.*

That was about right.

"You'll try to help her," she said. "You'll try." Her bracelets rang like coins.

She threw the last card, a helmeted rider, sword drawn, horse cantering. Suddenly she slid it under the other cards and placed them all behind her. She removed a chain bracelet from her wrist and lowered it slowly into his hand.

"Take this totem," she said. "Pain will destroy you—the old you—before it rebuilds. I'll pray for you. Remember, we're all links in the chain."

"Give me Luca," he said. "Tell me where he's going."

"I'll tell you," she said in a flat, even tone. "Because I trust you, Mr. Policeman, and I need you to save my brother. Will you help us?"

The candle in the overhead fixture stopped flickering and held as still as an arrowhead, as if awaiting his answer.

She trusted him. Or at least she believed in him, in his ability to save her brother. It wasn't because he was a policeman, but in spite of it. Her people had no use for the police. The police usually ran her people out of town. Her call, her request for help, hung in the stale air as he studied the sparkling chain in his palm and realized that deep down he did believe Luca Starbird was innocent—and not just because this astonishingly stunning woman said so. A warmth enveloped him, an electric surge of adrenaline. The emptiness, the void created by his ongoing failure to rehabilitate Lisa—*so much pain*—ached to be filled with the renewed purpose just such a mission would entail.

A mission of redemption, yes, for a soul who had lost his way.

He pocketed the chain, looked into her Gypsy green eyes, and nodded.

****

Later that night, fat raindrops plinked on Gerard's windshield like piano keys. He watched the Gypsy lot from his cruiser, watched Starbird's truck leave and drive past shuttered storefronts and postered walls. Rain fell faster and the truck's windshield turned white. At Gerard's signal, the cruisers on both sides of him flicked on their headlights. They were blocking the end of the street, and soon sirens blared and more patrol cars boxed the truck in from behind.

Gerard got out and stood in the pelting rain, raising his dripping hand and speaking as loud as he could. "The Commonwealth commits you to its custody, Luca Starbird."

Lightning flashed, thunder cracked. "The state of

Massachusetts arrests you for the murder of Alice Starke."

Troopers surrounded Starbird and held his arms. When he fought, more hands joined, pushing his head forward, forcing him to kneel. Water sluiced around his knees and climbed his thighs.

Gerard approached, crouched, and spoke. Adrenaline powered his words. "If there's some heathen god you're praying to, Starbird, save yourself the trouble, because the Real One is sharpening His sword."

They clamped manacles on Starbird's wrists and when he flexed his wet hands they looked as white as skeleton bones.

Chapter Fourteen

Angelo sat on the hood of his car in the parking lot of the County Correctional Facility. Sodium lamps flooded its walls and lighted guard towers sat on its corners. Dawn was coming—the start of Luca Starbird's first day in jail.

"How'd he get an arrest warrant?" Angelo growled. "This should have been our collar."

"Gerard has a phony witness who placed Luca in the rose garden after midnight," Conley answered. "Then all he needed was Starbird's long rap sheet and a well-paid judge."

Angelo hung his head. The sun was rising, sitting on the horizon like a half-eaten peach.

Conley sat next to him and sipped coffee. "There's no proof."

Angelo turned, his eyes narrowing. "Are you serious?"

"Gerard has nothing, Angelo."

"Starbird's rap sheet tells the story, Conley. He had a history and an opportunity, and when we show up he starts throwing knives and—" Angelo's eyes grew and he tilted his head back. "Damn, this is about his whore sister, isn't it? You let her seduce you. Christ, you're as big a deviant as her murdering brother."

The sun was full now. The lights at County Correctional powered off and Conley watched their glow slowly fade.

Conley's voice was resolute. "We've got nothing."

Angelo pounded the hood. "I'm telling you, Conley, Luca Starbird killed Alice Starke." His face hardened and his voice lowered to a rumble. "And so help me God, I'll be there when the judge puts that sorry bastard away."

****

Later that day, Gina watched a prison guard raise the spoon of tomato soup to his lips and slurp. When he was done he dragged his sleeve across his lips.

More soup. Dip. Raise. Slurp.

She watched him intently through the barred ticket taker's window separating them.

Dip. Raise. Slurp.

One of the others in the waiting room, an old woman, approached his desk. She had a round face with sunken eyes, gray-black hair pulled back tight from her moon face, and her scalp was sprinkled with dandruff that looked like confetti.

"Sorry to bother the sir," she said, yellow teeth smiling, "but I seem to have lost my chit." She shuffled and smiled wider. Her eyes sank deeper.

"I'm eatin'."

"I know, but the doors open soon and the pass you gave me is gone, and I need to see my Tommy."

Slurp.

"I'll be wantin' another," she said, voice quavering.

He laid the spoon on the desk, folded his hands, and closed his eyes.

"Here's the problem," he said. "I give you a new chit, then everyone will want one."

82

"I won't tell."

"They'll find out, oh, they will. They always do." He leaned toward the window grate. "Miscreants like youse can't hold secrets like that."

"I can, I can. Lordie, I can."

"If I start issuing extra tickets," he said, "next we'll get unauthorized visitors. Renegades, outlaws. And with that we can't abide."

She stiffened. "My Tommy needs fortification. Needs to see his mother. He's just a boy."

The guard nodded slowly. "Tell you what I'll do, sweetheart."

Her face brightened and her chin rose.

"I'll give you a promise and some advice," he said. "I guarantee Tommy will be right here in prison next Saturday when you come back. And next time I give you a chit, hold it tight. Pretend St. Peter gave it to you."

He found his smile. She lost hers and drifted slowly back to the exit.

Back to the soup, one eye on the crowd.

Gina walked to the counter. He dabbed his lips with a paper napkin.

"You're new," he said.

She nodded. "Gina."

"I'm the keeper of this little menagerie, dearie. The name's Perkins. We got a system here. You need a pass from me to see an inmate."

He waved her to the side door of his tiny office, removed magazines from a chair, and slapped his hand on the cracked leather seat. She sat. He turned a page in his journal and found a blank line.

"Who you here to see, my dear?"

"Luca Starbird."

"Ah, yes, our new guest. The lady killer."

He wrote carefully in the block on the form, laid the pen in the spine of the book, leaned back, and cracked his knuckles.

"You'll see prisoner Starbird through a thick glass. That's protocol. You'll talk to him through a phone on the wall. Better wipe the mouth and earpiece. No telling who used it last."

He wheeled closer and their knees almost touched. She didn't move, but watched him talk, staring at his mouth, anticipating the words he spoke.

"But we can do something about that, my lovely."

His hand covered her knee. She didn't flinch.

"I can even get you past the glass, sweetheart, if that's what you want." He retrieved a red ticket from a shelf and placed it in her palm. "Just let me know."

A buzzer blared and the others in the waiting room stood and queued in front of a steel door.

"Thank you for the kindness," she said.

She looked back once and saw him leering at her backside as she exited his office, on her way to the prisoner visiting room.

Chapter Fifteen

Gina looked up from her hard chair.

A glass wall divided the prisoner visiting room. Handprints decorated the barrier, white whorls left by splayed fingers and pressed palms. Smudges on both sides of the glass mirrored each other as if they were trying—aching—to connect. An oval of lipstick pouted at her from the divider, a candy-red kiss that seemed to be the only color in the room.

The inmate side was quiet save for prisoners' whispers into black wall phones and the occasional scrape of chair legs. Behind her, workers were finishing a clean-and-scrub for visitors' day and the stink of ammonia filled the room.

Luca nodded at her from the other side of the glass. He seemed calm and resigned as he folded his hands on the clean counter in front of him. The counter on her side was carved with graffiti, an upside-down collage of messages and drawings.

SHARON LUVS U

The cuttings looked new. The raw, damaged wood was the color of flesh.

ROT IN THIS HELL

She picked up the phone and spoke to her brother.

"Be patient, Luca. We have a friend, a policeman named Conley who will help us."

He stared into her eyes, his dark eyes flaring.

"Gina, what's wrong with you? Stay away from *gadjo* policemen. Their lies will kill us."

"No, he's a good man. I can tell. He believes us and he'll help."

Luca squinted. "Gina, I see the look in your eyes. You've fallen for this *gadjo*. Just like when you were a teenager, you've fallen. You look like a lovesick fool. Pura will be heartbroken, think of that."

She looked down and shook her head. Had she been so transparent? She thought of the policeman fondly, his zeal, his honesty, his caring, and her brother had sensed it.

A loud voice suddenly drowned her brother's words. A guard—Perkins again—spoke to a prisoner farther down. She heard a boy's low talk…and then Perkins spoke, loud enough for all to hear.

"Santini bothering you again, Tommy? I'll ask the cooks to saltpeter his meal. That should slow him down. Eh? No, your mother didn't come. Probably busy. The old girl might show up next week. Or maybe not."

The guard stopped next to Luca and smiled at Gina.

"I see your wife found you, Starbird."

Perkins' uniform stretched across his waist, squeezing his flesh into rolls and bunching his pockets.

"She's not my wife," Luca said.

Tommy rocked back and forth. Faster. Faster.

"Girlfriend?" Perkins asked Luca.

"My sister," Luca said.

"Sister," Perkins said, rubbing his hand over his mouth as if tasting the word.

Tommy's chest was heaving now. He breathed

rapidly, as if priming some internal engine. His hands started to tremble and his eyes rolled upward.

Visitors next to Gina rose and pointed, gasping. Perkins ignored the urgency behind him and spoke to Luca. "I can get messages to your sister, Starbird. I'll arrange a meeting perhaps. And just maybe you'll get a special meal tonight to seal the deal."

A female guard burst through the door and ran to Tommy. His hands were bent inward now, like straining claws. The tendons were white as bone.

"If you like," Luca said.

Thump.

Tommy hit the floor, legs bent in a fetal curl.

"Perkins!" the woman called, "we need to bring him to the hospital."

"The lad's hyperventilated again," Perkins answered. "Put him back in his cell. Santini will have an easier time getting at him."

Another guard joined her and they dragged the boy across the floor by his armpits. Tommy looked like a marionette, limbs jerking.

Perkins nodded calmly. "So it's set, Starbird. We'll arrange a meeting with Gina. You can look forward to her comfort. I'll see to it personally."

****

In another place, or perhaps another time, Captain Roland Gerard might have been less of a man. Would a spineless father have made him weaker? Would a mother less obsessed with nutrition have made him feeble? Would an accident, disease, or simple bad luck have formed him into the dreg who sat in front of him? Death was preferable.

The prison guard named Perkins sat on the edge of

the open ambulance and folded his arms over his fat belly.

"It wasn't my fault," he insisted, voice trembling. "It wasn't—"

Gerard raised his hand. "Tell me what happened—and just what happened. How did Starbird escape?"

Perkins composed himself.

"Here's how it was. They was screaming, which ain't unusual in the lockup. They're always singing some song in the cellblock at night, goes along with them rattling bars and thrashing sheets. But this song was different. Almost knocked me off my stool. So I retrieved my nightstick and flashlight from the desk."

"Did you know it was Starbird?"

"No. Well, I suspected it was. Fresh fish always scream the loudest. So I went down the corridor with my stick and my light. Most of the miscreants were in their bunks, peaceful for a change. I banged some of the bars, just to let them know I wasn't happy.

"I caught two pervs in C-block getting romantic, their faces touching, all sweaty and shiny." Perkins grimaced. "Old man Tinny was in the neighboring cell, sitting on the floor, rocking to some imagined sound."

We're wasting precious time.

"Get on with it," Gerard said and looked at his watch. "Tell me what happened, faster."

Perkins shook his head and continued.

"Then I heard another blood-curdling scream. A cough, a sputter, and a groan—just ahead. I almost slipped on a puddle of blood on the floor tiles. A hand brushed my face, and greasy fingertips tapped my cheek. Starbird was hugging the bars, his red arms sticking through. Blood poured from his mouth and nostrils, and wet his shirt. His eyes were glassy and his hair a mess. I grabbed his hand. "Lay down," I said. "Lay down, Starbird. You've hemorrhaged."

"He sank slowly, his arms sliding down the bloody bars. His knees hit the floor with a thud. I knelt on the other side and said, 'You'll live, Starbird, you'll live.'"

Gerard closed his eyes. *Delusions of valor, a simpleton who thinks he's a hero.*

"Then I ran to my office," Perkins said, "and when I lifted my phone, my hand slid in the wetness of the Gypsy's blood. I remember the feel." Perkins looked up, beseeching, as if seeking understanding—or pity. "That's what had me so damn convinced."

"I rode inside the ambulance, next to Starbird's gurney. The wail of the siren sounded distant, unreal from inside. When they took a sharp corner, we both was thrown against the wall. Starbird's limp body simply rolled and when it settled back, his cold arm rested against mine, and the chill gave me goosebumps. The ambulance slowed and I knew we'd arrived because its underside bottomed on the steep ramp to County Hospital Emergency.

"Starbird's hand twitched, so I touched it and felt a flutter. If there was still life in him, if he weren't already dead, if he still had breath in him, maybe they'd say I was…you know, commendation-worthy or something…saving his ass so he could be brought to justice. I threw open the back door and hustled out. The light from the emergency room was blinding, and the driver yelled something behind me, but I just ran through the entrance, grabbed an orderly and dragged him back toward the electric doors. I ordered him to help us with the stretcher and get us a room, pronto, no paperwork or questions. Just a sawbones to save Starbird."

"You left a prisoner unattended? That's aiding and abetting, you idiot! Christ, man, what were you *thinking?*"

But Perkins just sat there, shaking his head. "I got back to the entrance, and that damn light was so blinding—"

"And while you were gone, you stupid ass, he knocked out the paramedics and escaped. You've abetted a *murderer,*" Gerard interrupted, holding up a thin, bloody stir straw in a plastic evidence bag. One end had been scraped to a sharpened point. "The bastard drew his own blood, and now he's on the run again."

He retrieved his coat from a chair, and headed for the door before he turned. "Commendation, fuck. Say goodbye to your pension, moron."

Chapter Sixteen

In another part of the hospital, two rowboats sat on still water in an oil painting. One boat was pale salmon, the pink God used for sunsets. The other was the blue-green of tarnished copper. An island sat in the distance, with an emerald mountain in its middle, circled by an apron of beach and sand.

A doctor came out of the double steel doors under the boat painting—the entrance to the intensive care unit.

"This way," he said to Conley.

They left the waiting room and entered the doorway into the acrid reek of antiseptic. Lisa's sister had found her unresponsive and called Conley at work. He'd never felt so alone, so helpless.

"You're the husband?" the doctor said.

"Yes, this is a shock, Doctor. Only a few weeks ago, we were at the beach, but she started…regressing."

"She told me."

A hallway stretched before them.

"She spoke to you, Doctor?"

"A bit. She was drifting in and out."

"Is she talking? Can she hear?"

The doctor stopped at a door and placed his hand on the knob. A hum buzzed from the other side.

"I don't know. She doesn't speak anymore. Doesn't seem to hear either, but we have no way of telling. A hundred years of modern medicine and we still don't know when the brain is listening."

They entered. Lisa lay on a bed with white linens. Her hands were clenched as if she were holding a tow rope. Tubes curled all around her, connecting mouth and arms to machines. The control panel's lights played on her skin and made the tubes shine like silver.

A slender hose snaked from her mouth, hissing air that seemed to be coaxing that beautiful smile, the one that never needed coaxing. A machine chimed fast, like a tolling bell. The doctor hurried to a display and turned a knob. The tube to her arm dripped clear liquid that fell slowly.

Suddenly there was loud beeping, and the doctor swore, then hustled to the IV bag and twisted a lever. Drops fell faster.

Something was wrong. The day Matt had feared would arrive was here.

"Can she hear me?" he said.

"I believe she can."

Conley bent close and curled her hair behind her ear, his touch gentle.

More alarms chimed, faster, ringing like slots in a casino. The doctor shot out of the room as Conley lowered his face to her rigid hands and they started to loosen. Her face became slack and her skin seemed to pale.

"Take the pink boat, babe," he said, her cold wedding ring against his hand, "because it's as pretty as you are."

****

Conley opened the hospital's front door and stepped outside just before dawn, into a moonlit night with glimmering stars. He couldn't grieve. Lisa had just passed, but the loving Lisa he cherished had left long ago. Should he have been harder on her—or kinder? Angelo would certainly have an opinion. Regardless, he'd failed. A cicada-like buzz began in his head.

Father McCarrick approached from the parking lot, his hands folded. He wore a dark coat, shoulders hunched, and the sorrow in his voice was something Conley had never heard.

"Matt, I'm so sorry."

The words sounded distant.

"Let's pray, Matt."

The buzz in Conley's head grew louder, drowning out the words that droned from Father's mouth. They stood together, in one-sided prayer, and soon daybreak came. The stars blinked and disappeared as daylight crept over them.

"Matt, look at me, boy. Look at me. Listen to me."

A breeze started, and when a light rain began to fall, Conley realized he'd left his coat in Lisa's hospital room. He turned up his shirt collar, plunged his hands in his pants pockets, and felt cold metal. He drew the object out—the chain bracelet the Gypsy had given him—and the buzz in his head quieted as he remembered her words.

Pain will destroy you—the old you—before it rebuilds. Remember that, and remember—we're links in an ancient chain.

"Matt, I'm calling the doctor," McCarrick said. "You don't look well."

"No more doctors, Father. I'm okay."

Too much pain to bear. The Gypsy's jewelry rang like coins. *But peace follows.*

"Matt, you need time to grieve."

"Yes, Father."

The memory of Gina's words was insistent.

I trust you, Mr. Policeman. Trust me. Help my family.

Father McCarrick's face was shiny from the rain and his tired eyes bored into Matt's. "God's at work here. Everything has a purpose, Matt. Even this."

The rain stopped and the sky lightened. Conley put his arm around his old friend and led him to the parking lot.

"I know. Come on, Father. Let's put Lisa to rest."

Chapter Seventeen

The day after Luca escaped, a white blur spun past Gerard's head. Turned out to be Massachusetts. The sunshine state followed, then Nevada, Ohio, California. Mexico was the next license plate flung from the open door of the Gypsy camper. The plates clattered across the concrete, overlapping each other like thrown playing cards. The abandoned camper sat on rusted, tire-less wheels near the Ocean Park Industrial Center. Bumpers were stripped and window frames missing. Faded gray strips of aluminum lined its walls. The stink that drifted from inside was as rank as a festering wound.

State Trooper Novak appeared in the doorway and chucked another plate in the pile. He wore a kerchief against the camper's stench, a white hanky tied behind his neck and pulled over his nose. His dark eyes and tanned face looked like a coon's mask. He pinched the cloth on his nose and pushed it higher. His breath worked the cloth back and forth.

"That's all I found, Captain."

Gerard kicked the plates. "Now we know where they've been. Time to find where they're going."

Novak's eyes flickered toward the back of the trailer.

"Look some more," Gerard ordered.

Novak took a deep breath, then disappeared into

the trailer. Bangs and slams followed, and a sharp crunch. He called out.

"Captain, they left food. There's maggots."

Gerard ignored him and turned to the other men. Troopers and a few local cops were searching the lot. Two of them fit a long pry bar under the edge of a manhole cover, lifted, and peered inside.

Inside the trailer, Novak's sounds grew smaller—muffled sighs and groans. Detective Angelo crouched nearby. His open palm held hardened wax and cock feathers.

"Treasure, Angelo?"

More ruckus in the trailer. The camper shook as if from internal explosions.

"The treasure was Starbird, Gerard. The man you lost."

Now the men were opening a long grate with the pry bar. The metal rang and echoed when it fell on the pavement. Gerard studied them.

"Ever try to teach someone persistence and fortitude, Detective Angelo?"

"That's God's job—or the Devil's. I wouldn't offend either by trying."

Angelo collected more wax from a crevice and added it to his collection.

"Starbird can't hide forever," Gerard said. "No one can."

"Don't be so sure. They've split up. That's what they do to protect one another. You'll need to chase a hundred Gypsies. They'll see your army coming."

"No army needed. Luca Starbird's just a man."

The men at the grate hole were arguing now, talking over each other. The one with the pry bar lowered it into the opening until the bar disappeared. His hand followed it below the surface.

"Your partner Conley is on compassionate leave. You're unmatched, you two, because he's a plodder. And when he comes back from death leave, he'll be worse." Gerard lifted his chin toward the searchers. "We're not like them, you and me. We're warriors, persistent and strong. A small army. And we've got more luck than most. Our best chance of finding the Gyp is working together."

Gerard stuck out his hand. Angelo studied it.

Novak emerged from the door of the camper waving a tattered, unfolded map. His kerchief was down, replaced by a smile. He ran to them.

Angelo rose. Gerard leaned close to his shoulder and whispered.

"Starbird's just a man, Angelo. Just one man."

****

Everything was red.

Red light washed the walls and the incense smoke in the Boston massage parlor, and cast a crimson sheen over the two sarongs hung on the chair next to the massage table.

The smooth legs of the naked girls straddling Patrick Runyan's back and thighs were the color of ripe peaches. Their small hands massaged him and they mewled as they ground their sex into his skin. The languorous plink of a shamisen played from speakers.

When she saw Conley, one of the girls climbed off and left. The other one ignored him and worked harder, faster. She whimpered—eyes closed, face flush from orgasm—and climbed off.

Conley sat in a chair. Runyan opened his eyes.

"Do we have business, Detective Conley?"

"I hope so, Mr. Runyan."

The mamasan started a row with the girls outside the door. They spoke Vietnamese, fast and loud—staccato, then smooth. Their chatter sounded like song.

Runyan lifted himself onto his forearms and studied him. "Why so formal, Detective?"

Conley still wore the suit from Lisa's funeral that morning, and he could almost feel the handshakes of her well-dressed politician friends, and hear their insincere condolences. No need to explain to Runyan. It wasn't pertinent to the mission.

The music in the massage parlor was softer now, mostly flute. The women had retired to another part of the place and their distant voices sounded like the twittering of birds.

"How does one hire you, Mr. Runyan?"

Runyan pushed himself up, swung his legs over the table, and sat. His muscles rippled when he moved, and the swollen veins in his powerful arms looked like blue steel cords.

"Policemen can't afford me, Detective. At least honest ones can't."

"No worries." Conley fished Lisa's life insurance policy out of his coat pocket and showed him.

Runyan read the payout amount and raised one eyebrow. "What's the job?"

"Luca Starbird escaped County Correctional two days ago and disappeared," Conley said. "Help me find him. Help me prove his innocence."

"Why should I, and why is it so important to you?"

"You're a pragmatist, Mr. Runyan, a businessman. I'll pay whatever you say—if you want to be paid. You once asked me what it was like to be noble, to help someone you don't know. Here's your chance. I'm convinced Luca Starbird's been unfairly accused, and I've been asked to help, simple as that. Are you in?"

Runyan pushed his long hair back and stood. "Tell me more, Detective. Tell me everything."

****

Conley and Runyan spent the rest of July tracking the Gypsies. The trail was easy at first. The group had traveled north along the New England coast to carnivals and seaside amusement parks. Three days behind—a carnie remembered Pura selling potions in front of the Salisbury Beach Arcade. Two days out—tourists were still buzzing about Luca's knife throwing in Old Orchard Beach. They were only a day late when a breathless bartender in Boothbay Harbor described Gina's seductive smile as she stood in front of her fortune-telling tent.

Then it got harder. The large Gypsy caravan had split up somewhere north of Boothbay and gone a dozen separate ways, and Conley thought he knew why.

They know—they know we're following.

He and Runyan decided to follow a tip that led them inland, beyond Maine to New Hampshire, where the lush summer forest made the Granite State look like a fantasy land.

Michael Walsh

Part 2

Upcountry

Chapter Eighteen

"Problem with beauty is you gotta share it," Sheriff Joe Creighton said.

His fellow Officer Mike Harris grunted, planted a foot on a boulder at the edge of the overlook's parking lot, and folded his arms on his knee.

The New Hampshire Presidential Mountain Range stretched before them, bottle-green mountains against a bright blue sky. Their jagged peaks cast a shadow over the valley below that looked like a long, serrated blade. More mountains loomed in the distance under feathery clouds.

Cars pulled off the Kancamagus Highway into the lot. Radios blared through closed windows, along with baby cries, shouts, and laughter.

Creighton slapped the side of the wooden sign next to them. Letters carved with a mallet and chisel named the mountains. "It's already August. Autumn's coming," Joe said as he adjusted his cap and opened the cruiser door. "And winter. Half a year of cold and darkness soon."

"Slow down. Don't cut summer short, Joe. Best appreciate the few gifts this hard world gives."

The slam of their doors echoed like cannons across the valley. Faces stared at them through the grimy windows of the parked cars. Lately Creighton felt like he was just an actor in the hootenanny tour—hick cop only good for scaring bears away from dumpsters and setting speed traps in Mayberry.

"These visitors," Harris said, looking toward the mountains, "they aren't all bad. They bring something with them."

"Sure. Hamburger wrappers, Styrofoam cups—"

"Naw. We learn a little from every one, from every snotty-nosed kid, every fat, bored husband, every hippie."

"Things we don't need to know, Mike."

Harris shrugged. "They push us forward on the conveyor belt."

The cold was making Creighton's arthritis worse. He fit the key in the ignition, squeezed it between forefinger and middle finger, and turned. The key dug into his flesh, but he twisted hard anyway, the best he could, and the car started. The limitations of this disease seemed endless.

His brother complained of gout. A frog neck and occasional ankle lock? Big deal. Their dad had been hard of hearing. Why couldn't God have chosen that for him too? Hell, deafness was no mean disease. A boon really, a blessing to shut out half the horseshit a sheriff got fed every day from local punks and wisecracking tourists.

Instead, this curse.

Damn hand could barely work his zipper up after he took a leak. Goddamn hand was incapable of making a fist or holding a gun.

What kind of a cop is that?

Couldn't caress his wife the way she deserved. Couldn't even pleasure her anymore.

What kind of man?

Janet was the love of his life, and his granddaughter Dee-Dee was the light. He'd die for them. But how could he protect and provide when he couldn't even hold their hands? He'd give anything to have his health back. Anything.

They left the overlook and turned onto the Kancamagus. He rested his right hand on top of the steering wheel, gripping nine o'clock with his left.

Harris suddenly spoke.

"Maybe one of these new friends will bring us something valuable. Something we need."

"Or something terrible. Just as likely."

"No matter. They're coming, Joe. It's called progress."

"I got another name for it."

A van rumbled by and downshifted to make the climb. Easy to tell the outsiders. They fought the Kancamagus and had no idea how to use gravity.

Creighton's coffee cup steamed in the holder on the transmission hump. He should've taken a swig before they started. God knew he needed it. Steam rose from the hole he'd torn in the top. The aroma permeated the car, smoky and fresh. Funny how such a trivial thing as caffeine brought such pleasure.

They climbed the rolling highway. He turned his head and gazed out the window at moss-covered rocks and green foliage. The car seemed to be standing still, the landscape beside them traveling like a diorama on a moving treadway.

The top of the wheel felt like granite under his bum hand. He struggled with the left to keep the car steady. Easy on the brake on the down track—*use momentum for the incline.*

Harris glanced down at the coffee cups, raised his, and drank.

Was Mike looking at him? Watching the hand? Hard to tell what he was spying behind those damn shades. Was his partner worried a weak grip was the only thing keeping them on the narrow road? Or was he just wool-gathering, pining for the warmth of his wife and the glow of his wood stove?

Downhill. Creighton took his foot off the pedal and coasted. A big Kenworth crested the rise ahead, its grill sparkling in the sunlight. Smoke shot from the vertical exhaust pipe. Gears growled. The rig topped the hill fast and started the downward seesaw ride with more speed than it needed. He was pulling a flatbed of stacked metal bars with big red mushroom caps on top. Some kind of kiddie ride headed to the county fair in Lincoln. The folded beams made the contraption look like a kneeling spider.

The rig sped down the steep hill and suddenly its air brakes groaned. Sun streaked the windshield, hiding the moron who didn't appreciate the power under him.

Another asthmatic cry, more brake to slow the hurtling beast.

The second burst started it, just a waver at first, a wobble. The trailer started to come around, to twist on the cab's coupling. Then faster, especially when the brakes whistled a third time. The cargo—the spider legs—vibrated, the red saucers quivered. Tires chattered sideways, skidding and smoking. The rig swung like an opening door.

Creighton slowed. No shoulder beside them, nowhere to go. Just thick pine trunks and boulders. The jackknifing truck slid closer. Harris held his hands on the dashboard, elbows locked. Creighton's left hand, its knuckles white, squeezed the wheel. He tried to will the right one to life. The left started to ache. He tapped the brakes and wondered where he'd go.

The truck cab started to turn, pulled by the runaway load. A mushroom cap slid, threatening to break free.

Only yards away now, coming fast, impact imminent. Creighton turned toward the trees on his right, a copse of narrow saplings, and drove into them as the flatbed's pointed corner neared. The trees flew backward and metal scraped the length of the cruiser. The right fender struck bark and a headlight popped like a firecracker. Pine boughs flew, a flurry of green. Coffee spilled from the holder and scalded their legs. They lurched forward and struck again, a thick trunk this time, and their airbags burst open, then slowly deflated.

The truck passed and the cruiser stood tilted on the trunk it had climbed. The hood was crumpled like tissue paper, the windshield shattered into white veins. Harris was still braced against his airbag. Creighton saw the reflection of the bent truck in the rearview mirror, chattering to a stop, smoke rising from tires and cab.

"Tell me again about outsiders bringing bunches of good to the area."

His right hand started to shake and patter on the steering wheel, the only thing on the highway that seemed to be moving.

Suddenly Harris reached over and gripped Joe's hand tightly, and squeezed the fingers to stop the tremors. Creighton's heart felt like a drumbeat in his chest and the scream of metal rung in his ears. His partner spoke.

"We ain't dead yet, Joe."

Harris had a bloody gash on the side of his head and his wide eyes were as blue as the sky.

He said it again.

"We ain't dead yet."

Chapter Nineteen

The next day, Creighton patrolled the Grafton County Fair, watching, listening, and carefully keeping distance from his granddaughter Dee-Dee and her friends. She hated his over-protectiveness, but he didn't care. Abandoned by an uncaring father she never knew and orphaned by an uncaring mother who died from heroin, Dee-Dee would get special attention for the rest of her life, like it or not.

Dee-Dee's boyfriend Danny Murphy reared back, his bicep and shoulder muscles collecting. The cords in his neck grew and his left hand rose to cover the baseball in his right hand. Eyes opened wide, threatening the space before him. His long hair swirled and he threw. The arm snapped like a whip, hand sprung open, and the ball hissed forward like snake spit. Candlepins exploded from a pedestal and whacked the heavy tarp behind them.

"Awesome," his friend Billy Sampson opined.

Creighton's granddaughter rested her chin on the teddy bear she held, her arms circling its chest. He'd soon join panda, black bear, brown bear, and polar bear in her room. She kissed the curls on top of the bear's head.

Sampson's laugh cut the cold night. Corn kernels were stuck between his teeth, and dried ketchup gave him a dark goatee.

"Awesome," he repeated and laughed as though he'd just heard the punch line for a joke.

Probably stoned again.

Dee-Dee's friend Suzanne pressed against Sampson's shoulder and giggled with delight.

The kids walked on, searching for the next man challenge—water gun, ring toss, dart shoot.

Hay stirred under them on the dirt path. The bright lights of the booths on both sides lit the alley. Sampson gazed at the colored lights lovingly, his dilated pupils as big as coins. An air rifle banged and he jumped. Rock music blared. The smell of buttered popcorn filled the air.

A tent stood on their right, worn but fancy. A curved valance surrounded its edge, and red and green pennants streamed from its top. The blue door flap was covered with white stars and lazy slivers of moon. A single light flickered inside and made the walls almost opaque. An odd thing, that tent, stuck in a row of wooden booths filled with greasy, leering, jeering barkers.

"Show the ladies how it's done, sonny. Step right up."

Danny stopped at the basketball shoot, cradling one ball after another in his long fingers, flicking them toward the basket, waving after every one.

Creighton watched the barker stare at Dee-Dee's chest, cleavage, ass. She was struggling with her growing attraction to men—and their danger, and this time she studiously ignored the letch, just like Granddad taught her, and squeezed her bear until one of its eyes popped off. Before she could retrieve it, someone crushed the plastic disc under his foot, and the broken eye twinkled in the dark dirt.

Joe Creighton winced. Maybe he could get his wife to sew on another eye.

More games. Hammer the pad, lift the ball, ring the bell.

Finally, they moved beyond the glitz and noise. Other scents would assail them now—manure and feed, earthy and strong. They entered a barn through a big door, to the sounds of lows and bleats, baas and quacks. The cows standing in shallow stalls looked as lifeless as the medallions hung around their necks on blue ribbons. Fluffy sheep in a pen looked soft as pillows. Guinea pigs, pigeons, and rabbits stared from black cages.

Danny strolled past the critters. Suzanne wrinkled her nose. Creighton unobtrusively followed closer.

Suddenly they stopped and watched a quivering ball of gray and white fur in a rabbit pen. One rabbit had mounted another. Sampson turned to Suzanne and laughed.

"They're fucking," he said, stretching the word until it sounded like he'd emptied his lungs.

Suzanne snorted and put her nose close to the cage, and Danny turned to Dee-Dee and smiled. Dee-Dee pressed her rosy cheeks harder against teddy.

She was safe for now.

Chapter Twenty

The Creightons' home had become a battleground the next morning, though now it was quiet and still. The house seemed diminished by their argument. The high-ceilinged great room had become small and confining—not so great. The fire in the stone fireplace, a roaring blaze when the battle began, was a dying carcass of embers glowing through white ash. Leaves floated outside, tittered against the windows, landed on the ledges, and built walls that looked like dark honeycombs against the glass.

Joe Creighton stood behind the kitchen counter, fished a spatula and cast iron pan from a cabinet, and waited for the next round to begin. Suddenly Janet was at the door, her arms loaded with firewood. Leo stood beside her, tongue hanging, tail wagging. Janet shouldered the door open, bee-lined to the fireplace, and stacked logs on the coals. The fire grew. Leo watched intently.

Janet turned and marched toward him with purpose. He cracked an egg into the pan and it hissed. Then another. He laid three strips of bacon around the edges.

"We can't let Dee-Dee stay out all night. The girl's too young," he said.

"She'll be fine. Trust me on this one."

His bad hand ached this morning. He'd have to

work the eggs with his left. *Southpaw eggs. Wonder if they'll taste the same?* The wide yellow yolks stared back at him.

"Nothing good happens after midnight, Janet."

"My job's worrying about bad things, Joe, and I guarantee nothing bad will happen."

Leo's head turned back and forth between them. A long string of drool stretched from his mouth to the wood floor.

"Why can't you respect my opinion for a change?" he said.

"I respect your opinion, I just disagree with it."

The bacon lifted and sizzled. Grease splattered onto the stovetop. Leo snapped to attention, pattered to his master, and sat on his shoe.

"You're a good woman, Janet, but you're soft-hearted when it comes to Dee-Dee. She needs tough love."

"She's had more than her share of tough love in this life."

"Can't think like that. It's called pity and it's a cancer."

Every marriage had its wars. Thirty years of police work had taught him that. Truth be told, he and Janet probably fought less than most and their spats never lasted long, at least when Kim was alive. The day their daughter died, a day that cleaved their lives into the Before and After, their granddaughter Dee-Dee became the focus of their world. Raising her brought consternation, worry, and heartache.

"Maybe if you retired like a proper old man, you'd be around to help more with Dee-Dee."

She reached out, open handed. Truce? Had the tide

turned? He placed his right hand in hers. How would this skirmish end? There were many possibilities, ranging from capitulation to a kind of twin amnesia where they both pretended nothing had ever happened.

"Maybe we'd just battle more," he said.

"Maybe not. We only fight about Dee-Dee. She'll be grown up and gone before you know it."

A gust of wind howled outside. The leaves came faster.

"Sunnyside or over easy?" he said.

"Quit that," she said. "Don't change the subject. Young ladies stay out late on Harvest Dance night. It's done all the time these days, a rite of passage."

"These days are no different from those days."

She took a step toward him.

"Sunnyside," he said, nodding at the pan. "Maybe it'll help your disposition."

She squeezed his hand. "Joe, it's no picnic bringing up a teenaged girl. You could help more."

"Maybe I could."

He lifted the eggs onto a plate, yolks still intact. Set the bacon on a paper towel. She slid onto a stool.

"What's that mean, Joe Creighton?"

"Change ain't an easy thing, Janet. Even good change. Requires some resolve, a little stubbornness maybe."

"No more riddles."

"Maybe I'm talking about retiring. That decision is a big riddle in my mind if you want to know the truth."

"Think about us together every day," she whispered. Her hair fell over her eye, sexy, like an old-time movie starlet. "Like kids."

He shook his head. "Too much of a good thing is

usually the death of it."

"Doesn't have to be. Passages are never easy, Joe. Oftentimes they're not a choice. With God's help we'll get through."

He tried to squeeze her hand, but his barely moved. She didn't seem to notice.

He smiled. "God doesn't seem to be much of a help these days. But He's always been reliable at telling me when it's time to move on."

****

Good ending to this little war, even though resolution still seemed distant and the Fall Harvest Dance was just a week away.

They lay in bed together that night, wrapped in silk sheets, listening for Dee-Dee to come home. Janet's flesh was warm, soft, smooth, same as when they were young. Even in the autumn of their lives, the thrill hadn't gone. Janet drew her leg around his, cupped the back of his shoulder with her hands, and pulled him close. The sheets sluiced between them, bound them together, and became part of the embrace.

Janet attacked sex like she did life—with passion and strength. When they were done, they were kids again—the boy from upcountry who checked out his shoes whenever he talked to the opposite sex, and the girl from Derry who always smiled when she spoke.

A knock on the door, insistent pounds. The sun was rising, they'd fallen asleep embracing. He was about to throw off the covers, but first he passed his hand the length of his wife's silk legs. She smiled at him mischievously, and suddenly her hands travelled too and her hips lifted toward him.

Sweet Jesus.

The loudness again, sharp hurried raps that had the clarity of a church bell.

He stepped into his pants and walked bare-chested into the great room. Mike Harris stood outside, cheeks red, brow sweating. Creighton opened the door and his deputy stepped inside. Leo stirred from his place next to the fire and opened sleepy eyes.

"It's Dee-Dee," Harris said and stood so close his coffee breath washed Creighton's face. Harris removed his hat and worried the brim with both hands. Tears formed in the corners of his glassy eyes.

"Oh, God, Joe, come quick. It's Dee-Dee."

Chapter Twenty-One

On the third day of August, Runyan found two of the Gypsy clan after a scorched earth campaign that left a trail of trembling informants. Conley demanded there be no violence, and Runyan answered with steel blue eyes, but obeyed. In a seedy motel room near Portsmouth, Conley knocked on the door and showed his badge to a Gypsy couple. Runyan took the man into the bathroom to interrogate.

The woman sat on the motel bed, as still as the blond headboard decorated with carved pineapples. Tears coursed her plump brown cheeks. Her arms opened, beseeching, and her fists pounded her chest. The bedsprings complained.

"He knows nothing," she said to Conley. "Please, Mister, let him go." Her nose ran and she dabbed a ball of white tissue to one nostril, then the other. "You're a good man," she confided. "Help my husband and I'll cast you the spell for good life. I swear." She pressed the wet tissue against her eyes.

She'd do anything to save her husband, she said. Or would she? The words turned to sobs. "He won't hurt your husband," Conley said. "I guarantee it. We want to help Luca. Where is he?"

The sound of running water stopped. A cry sounded. They looked at the stripe of light showing under the bottom of the bathroom door. "You don't understand. Luca's the Devil," she said, voice straining. Blue veins heaved under her brown skin.

"Tell us where he is."

A cry came from the bathroom where Runyan was questioning the man, followed by begging. The Gypsy man's sobs were a battle call to his wife, loud and shrill, and she stiffened.

"We'll give you anything," she said. "Money. Women."

Her husband whimpered on the other side of the door.

Suddenly she turned and spoke mechanically, as though his words had turned a crank. Her voice had a hard, guttural edge.

"We will kill you then," she said to Conley. "A terrible death for you and the monster. You'll die together."

He shrugged. "All right, but first—give us Luca."

****

Lisa again—her specter—appeared to Conley, summoned maybe by the silhouette of the girl strolling between a broken picket fence and a dark stand of pines outside the motel. Lisa was visiting more often. *Or was it Gina?*

Paper rustled and crackled. Runyan was unfolding a map on the hood of the car and smoothing it with his walnut knuckles and rope-veined hands. A thick finger poked a spot near the top of the map.

His eyes were bright, hands steady. His finger traced a red-line highway on the map, past green places. "He's here," he said, fingertip parked in the middle of gray ripples that marked mountains.

A racket started behind them. The Gypsies pulled

out of the lot in a rusted station wagon, and gravel pelted their wheel wells.

Runyan ignored the sound and studied the map route. Conley envied him—a man with a purpose-driven life, supremely confident, and comfortable in his own skin.

As opposed to one haunted by a dead wife and obsessed with redeeming a man he hardly knows.

Conley stepped forward. His finger followed a faint line that approached the gray mountains from the side. "I know the place. Here. Take this road. A fast route with little traffic. It ends in a long curve, right in the middle of town."

Runyan reached in his pocket and held out a dangling set of keys hung from a chain attached to a brown rabbit's foot.

"Take the wheel," he said and put the key into Conley's hand. "You're the boss."

Chapter Twenty-Two

Grief is a ladder—a tall one.
Creighton and his wife had climbed its first rung together when their daughter Kim died. Pure pain—distilled, acute, debilitating. The second step was numbness, a merciful crosspiece that presented itself when the anguish became unbearable.

But this?
This was past pain, past unfeeling, Creighton thought as he followed Mike Harris to the crime scene. He felt out of body, incorporeal. He'd reached the end of the ladder, top rung. Sweet mercy transported him to the canopy of the cool woods, high above the damp woods trail, past the dark leaves that filtered sunshine. He hovered and felt the sun on his back, unfiltered. He looked down and saw himself and Mike Harris walking the path to the glen. Mike's thin hair didn't hide the whiteness of his bald spot, and his hunched shoulders made him look simian.

They walked across the flat rocks covering the trail. Tourists stumbled on them because of their unevenness, but locals knew to pick each rock carefully, as if choosing game pieces. Movement ahead—blue and brown uniforms showing through the trees. They stepped off the trail, into the green glen, to a blue blanket that lay before them.

The techs walked around the blue cover, writing,

talking, taking pictures. They were boys really, brave souls called to a job few aspired to. Most of their work came from car wrecks, carnage on the interstate, hulks of twisted metal so mangled you never knew what kind of surprise waited inside. Occasionally they were called to recover the corpse of a fallen mountain climber, maybe an amateur unfit for the four-thousand footers, or a pro whose luck had run out.

He knelt.

Dee-Dee didn't deserve to meet these boys. She wasn't driving recklessly on a hairpin curve or climbing a killer mountain. She was just being a girl.

Harris knelt next to him and pulled back the blanket. Creighton's breath stopped.

I'm not here, I'm above.

Dee-Dee lay on her side. Twigs extended from her once-beautiful eyes. Her face was white and her pursed lips were pink. Creighton flinched and his chest heaved. His legs felt weak, as if the effort of climbing the trail had finally demanded its due.

"Joe, you okay?" Harris said.

A camera flashed from behind, just over their shoulders. A tech had taken a picture of his beloved Dee-Dee. The flash bleached her pale skin and burned the image into Creighton's memory—not that he'd ever forget.

He looked above, past the canopy. Might as well be him and Janet down there under that blanket with their granddaughter because now they were incorporeal too. Statues, automatons, puppets that moved arms and legs, inhabitants of a heated house that would now become a permanently cold place. And if nothingness was to be their lot, then so was any chance of happiness, because sorrow and joy were the twin, inseparable promises of this life.

Dee-Dee.

Enough. He stood and scoured the glen, looking for clues and evidence, considering her killer, talking to the techs, reading their notes. Even a broken heart kept pumping blood.

When they were done, he looked at the sky again and imagined himself riding one of the white cotton clouds like a kid on a sled, hanging over its edge and enjoying the scenery. He and Harris left beloved Dee-Dee under the blue blanket in the glen and headed back to the trail.

And he worried the ladder of grief might have more rungs than he thought.

****

Later that day, a hammer chocked behind Creighton and Dee-Dee's friends—the last people to see her alive. Ropes slackened and whipsawed as the carnies broke down booths and stands. Gray-shirted men worked, cigarettes hanging from their mouths, smoke rising from their serious faces. Wooden walls fell, clapping against each other. They stirred a breeze, a sour whiff of wood.

Sampson stood on Danny's right, Suzanne on his left. Creighton could hear their breathing. Sampson suddenly spoke.

"Sorry for your loss, Sheriff. Sorry about Dee-Dee."

Creighton lowered his head and nodded. He looked up. "How 'bout you, Danny? You sorry for my loss too? She was your girl."

Chock. Chock. A man dragged a wide board past

them, and its edge dug a long trench in the rich black soil.

"Of course I am."

"Yes, sir would be the appropriate answer," Creighton said.

"Yes, sir."

"What happened last night?"

"We went to the fair again, and afterwards we all stopped at the hamburger joint near your house. Dee-Dee didn't want to eat, said she was tired, so she just walked home. That's all we know."

"And you let her?"

Danny's mouth opened and closed before his eyes turned glassy. He looked away. Creighton walked past him and considered the abandoned booths.

"Let's take a walk," he said to the group. "The same walk you all took with my granddaughter."

He turned and they followed single file, feet kicking the dirt furrows. They passed what was left of the duck booth—a long iron tub filled with black water and yellow plastic ducklings. Ring toss next, a plywood bed that held blocks collared with bright rings.

Danny stayed three paces behind. When they all suddenly stopped, Sampson bumped into Suzanne and she pushed him away.

"These men," Creighton said, wagging two stiff fingers of his bad hand at the workers. "Any of them talk to Dee-Dee?"

"They talked to everyone, Sheriff," Suzanne said. "Yelled mostly, selling their games."

His head swiveled slowly to the right and stopped at Danny.

"Any of 'em leave an impression?"

Danny shook his head. "Not especially."

Forward again. Dusk was settling and the cigarettes of the workers glowed like tracers, red beacons against darkening faces. They came to an empty lot on the right, a lightened square of trampled grass. Something different about it.

"What was here?" Creighton said.

"Don't remember, Sheriff."

Creighton reached out and snagged the forearm of one of the carnies. "Help me out. What kind of game booth leaves a bruise like that?"

The man stared at the pale grass, hesitated, and ran a hand down his face.

"Gypsy," he said softly, slowly, as if the word were climbing back into his memory. "Gypsy tent." Faster, louder. "Man and a woman inside, doing their magic. Nice looking bitch."

"Where are they? Do you know?"

He took a long drag of cigarette before he spoke. The ember grew.

"Not with us. They were passing through and rented the open space, that's all."

Suzanne stepped forward. "The fortune teller. I remember. She opened the tent flap and looked at me, but I didn't look back. My Gram says they can't throw a curse if they don't see your eyes."

Creighton kneaded his bad hand with his good. "Where'd they go?" he said to the worker.

"I'd check the campgrounds, Sheriff, or the woods. Strange people, them Gyps." He puffed thoughtfully on his cigarette and exhaled a lungful of smoke. "They like to be alone, they do. Rather spend time with plants and animals than with decent human beings."

Chapter Twenty-Three

A man-high pumpkin graced the lawn of the Story Land Motel in North Conway, New Hampshire, a bulbous plaster jack-o-lantern. Scabs of orange had flaked off, revealing white. Angelo flicked his cigarette into the grinning mouth and it pinged inside and echoed.

Light flickered and hummed on the neon motel sign overhead. Dark silhouettes of gingerbread houses, a teacup ride, and a carousel loomed in the amusement park next door. The outside of the motel was stucco in a harlequin pattern—some patches were yellowed with water damage, others darkened with mold. Window shutters cut into butterfly wings, blue with red spots. Rusted wires—bug antenna—arced from the top of the window.

Gerard shuffled behind Angelo on the yellow brick walk. They'd searched a dozen places marked on the map from the abandoned trailer in Ocean Park, and they were nearing the last location left. Luca had to be there.

They came to the entrance, brown planks banded together with iron straps to look like a castle door. A gold ring hung on the middle. Gerard was reaching for it when Angelo spoke.

"Why are we staying here?"

Gerard turned his palms up.

"Nothing available in Lincoln. It's high season in

the upcountry."

Angelo grunted, bent his arm, and hammered the bottom of his fist against the latch. The door flung open.

The lobby was filled with people talking and laughing. Some sat in grotesque chairs with plastic human-shaped arms and legs. Clerks hustled back and forth behind the check-in counter, the tails of their tuxes swishing. Their oversized red bowties seemed to float in front of them. A pair of glockenspiels sat on the mantel over the desk, backlit, shining golden stripes on counter and customers.

Gerard spied a Lincoln newspaper on the check-in counter whose headline shouted MURDER. He unfolded the paper, read, and showed it to Angelo.

"It could be him," Gerard said and turned to a desk clerk with wire-rimmed glasses.

"I need the number to the Lincoln Sheriff's Office."

"For an emergency?" the clerk asked.

"Not anymore."

The clerk hurried to the back room and returned with the number. A woman stood at the counter near Angelo, smoothing her blond hair with a delicate hand, studying him. He studied back. Interesting cat, that Angelo. Women couldn't take their eyes off his thick, slicked hair, his dark, beard-shadow face, his jet-black eyes, and he stared back at them like they were zoo animals. Maybe that's why they liked him.

Gerard punched the Sheriff's Office number into his cell phone and it started ringing.

The glockenspiels overhead came to life and banged sharp notes. The blonde grinned like a cartoon cat, winked at Angelo, and spoke to him.

"Gonna visit the amusement park, Slick? What are you boys into—princesses or fairies?"

Angelo slid his hand over her shoulder and down her arm, slow and sensuous. He had a way of making an innocent touch look dirty.

"We ain't interested in gentle things, sweetheart. We're here to catch a monster."

****

At dusk, Pura searched his canvas bag, dragging his tired hand along the rough bottom, and found the last few mushrooms with his fingers. They were babies—with rubbery, round fans under the heads, and stems as soft as skin. He quartered them, pushing the jackknife against his thumb, and flicking the morsels into the pot. The fire under the pot crackled, and he threw grass on top of the boil to dampen the steam. He inspected his thumb, hardened and scarred.

Gina brought firewood, knelt next to him, and laid the wood in crosses on the campfire. He stirred the pot hanging over it with a stick.

There was movement in the big pine to the right. Luca emerged from the trees, and the flame of the campfire distorted him like an apparition before he disappeared into the van. He returned and sat between them, and she rested her head on his shoulder. He opened a ruled pad on his lap and drew a curving line with a piece of charcoal, drawing quickly, as if his mind's eye were in danger of losing details. Mountain. Woods. Trails. Their van, tent, even the nearby trees. His hand darted over the pad, lifting every time he crossed the notebook's spiral. He shaded the mountain. Finally he slowed and his eyes softened. Pura looked into the fire and murmured a prayer.

Luca showed Pura the map.

"*Gadjos* are coming," Pura said and ran his hand down his face. The thumb sounded like a stone when it scraped against his beard stubble. He stirred the pot. "Let's prepare to greet them."

Chapter Twenty-Four

Waiting—for the sun to rise and the mist to melt.

Waiting—for two cops from the city, Angelo and Gerard.

Waiting—to kill the bastard who murdered Dee-Dee.

Creighton sipped his coffee at the Jigger Johnson Campground off the Kancamagus Highway. Leo stirred in the passenger seat and the golden curls on his sleeping body heaved.

Creighton sipped more coffee. Leo snored.

Maybe the Gypsy Luca would run when they found him. Maybe Creighton would have a chance to put a bullet between his shoulders and save the state of New Hampshire the electricity required to cook the son of a bitch.

His deputies sat nearby in the parking lot. Tom Owens looked ghostly behind the fogged window of his Ford. He'd bought the canary-yellow convertible the day after his divorce, a long, sleek job with a black rag top, but he never looked right in it. It would take more than a sexy car to recapture Tom's youthful magnetism.

Jerry Bush was sleeping behind his steering wheel, crew-cut noggin dipping forward and springing back every few seconds. Jerry's jarhead matched his boxy import. Both were square as a takeout box from China Garden.

The moon was almost gone over the horizon. Hard to tell if its dying light was illuminating boulders on Mount Chocorua or if the rising sun was introducing a new day.

A car rumbled into the lot and Leo popped an eye open. It held two men—more outsiders. Creighton thought of them as tourists even though he knew they were lawmen from the city. They got out and stood in the dirt lot. He guessed the older one with brown, cop-issued shoes—scarred and worn—was Gerard. His partner's shoes were shiny as river rocks.

Angelo.

The old man, puffy-eyed and slow, took time to adjust, to stretch and blink. Angelo peered at the tents in the campground.

Creighton finished his coffee and got out. Leo leaped out and stood beside him. The sky was turning purple and the skeletal outlines of scrub pines showed in the distance near Mount Washington. The tents in the campground lightened and became more yellow than gray.

Gerard approached holding an eight-by-ten photo in front of him like a proclamation. Creighton's deputies stepped closer and studied it. Creighton walked to the back of his car, opened the trunk, and lifted out his deer rifle. Leo danced when he saw it.

"Here's our man, boys," Gerard told them, loud, clear, commanding. "Sorry for your loss, Sheriff, but you're on the right track. The same filthy Gypsy killed a girl named Alice Starke in Massachusetts, same M.O."

Creighton ignored him, stepped between the deputies and Gerard, and took command.

"Tom, you take half the men and follow the trail north of the campers. Jerry, take the south trail."

Leo sniffed the ground around Angelo and licked the polished shoes.

"The manager says he put the Gypsies at the far site," Creighton said, "away from families. There's only one direction out and you're looking at it. Other way has a mountain a goat couldn't climb."

Gerard scratched the back of his neck. "Let's talk about this, Sheriff."

Creighton switched his rifle to his good hand and turned to Gerard. "We just did. The trails are clearly marked. They end at the Gypsy site. Stay hidden. Apprehend Mr. Luca if he runs. Leo and I are going in through the middle of the campground. I'll talk to the Gyps, see if we can do this peaceably."

"I'll go with you," Angelo blurted.

Fast talker, this Angelo—anxious to get the words out, as if his brain couldn't hold them for long. Those hurry-up words had an interesting effect on Leo. The dog's tail stopped wagging and hung still.

"No," Creighton said. "It'll be just me and Leo."

Angelo leaned forward and his aftershave cut the sweet morning air like a razor.

"I'm gonna need some time alone with Luca, Sheriff."

Persistent prick, used to his own way. Creighton patted Leo, smiled, and answered.

"Get in line."

Creighton set off toward the camps. The deputies dispersed and retrieved guns from their cars. They strapped on holsters before they headed for their assigned trails, whispering. Angelo's head swiveled back and forth before he started after the deputies taking the north trail. Gerard followed.

The campground was still. There were sleepy voices in a few of the tents—early morning risers. Tight sacks of food hung from ropes—bear hangs. Leo stood under each one, studying and sniffing.

They wound between tents and the black ash of dead campfires. Cans were strewn among them, along with cigarette butts and marijuana roaches. Snores rose from one tent. A sleeping bag zipper whisked in another. The contentious voices of a man and a woman muttered sleepily.

On both sides of the campground, the deputies made their noisy way in line formation. Flashes of tan shirts and dark jackets showed through the trees.

He and Janet used to camp, just the two of them in a small tent with a sagging roof an arm's length away. Isolated from the world, conscious of each other's every movement, of the warmth of each other's flesh, of every breath. And in that wonderful, sweet canvas prison, they'd pretend to sleep, and pretend they were the only people in the world. When the sun rose and lit the tent walls, and the morning sounds of other campers intruded, they'd finally rise. But he'd wished the night, and the long, sleepless dawn would continue forever. He could almost hear Janet's sweet, drowsy voice.

He touched the smooth, dew-wet top of a tent and stepped over its staked rope.

The woods got thicker. Tents were sparse now, fighting for space under a dense stand of trees. No picnic benches here. The weeds were higher than Leo. This was a rarely-used part of the place where campground managers exiled college kids, misfits, and bickering couples. A wall of pines seemed to mark the end of the campground, but Creighton knew there was a special reserve behind. It was barely a campsite, a hidden grove where Herb hid his most despised customers. He approached the pines. A dead campfire stunk like wet garbage.

Leo's curls rose on the back of his neck as Creighton pushed back the boughs to reveal a van and a tent. An old man sat on a log staring at the char of a dying fire, and a young woman had an arm around his shoulders. No sign of Luca. Creighton studied the van and tent, waiting for the killer to show himself.

Leo suddenly jumped through the opening and the old man and the girl lifted their heads and stared at them, unsurprised. Damn dog never did learn stealth. Leo bee-lined to an overturned pot and sniffed energetically. Creighton stepped through the trees and into the Gypsy camp sooner than he wanted to. He pointed his rifle at the van and stood in front of the blank-faced Gypsies, head high, eyes searching.

Chapter Twenty-Five

Gerard and Angelo followed their leader, a fat boy whose double chin jiggled like a bloated wattle. His belly stretched his parka and made his arms look skinny and weak. But he held his rifle well, this slug called Tom.

Country Tom.

He pointed the barrel toward the ground, swinging it in a slow, steady arc, and gripping the stock deftly in stubby fingers. His blue-clad brothers marched behind, their feet shuffling, their vacant eyes studying the trail as they lovingly cradled their weapons in their arms.

Gerard grinned.

Darwinian rejects. Chop a tree, shoot a deer, that's it, good job.

Morning dew dropped from leaves and made dirt cling to their boots. Voices drifted through the campground and filtered through dense trees. Sites became thinner, quieter. Soon they'd be abreast of Joe Creighton and the Gypsies. Angelo caught his eye and nodded. Gerard nodded in return. They needed to ditch these yokels. Suddenly Angelo wheeled left and pointed his gun at a row of staggered pines. Two of the boys lifted their rifles and vectored on the invisible target. All of them looked left. Pine tree boughs hid a narrow trail, an offshoot to the one they were on. Skeletal branches of bare trees reached toward the meager path like bony fingers.

Country Tom hurried to Angelo, huffing, sweating.

"What's your target?"

"It's him. He's in there. Luca." Angelo pointed with his chin. "He's wearing a light jacket, like a buckskin."

"Might be a camper," Tom protested.

Angelo shook his head. "No, it's not. I'm the only one here who's seen him, Constable, and I ain't one to forget a lady killer."

Country Tom exhaled deeply through his mouth. Angelo spoke. "Sheriff said 'Apprehend Mr. Luca if he runs,' Tom. Remember?"

Gerard watched Tom's eyes bore into Angelo's with surprising appraisal. Had they underestimated this Neanderthal? Would Country Tom challenge and show a glimmer of intelligence? Would he question why the others, all hunters and woodsmen, hadn't seen or heard the prey?

"We'll take care of it, Detective Angelo." Tom put his hand on Angelo's gun and lowered it slowly. "You got no range with that thing anyway."

Then he waved to the others, an open-handed come-on, and pointed at the trail. The lemmings scurried silently toward the unseen target, but he stopped the last man.

"Yancey, go tell Sheriff Creighton what we got."

"No," Gerard interrupted. "Angelo and I will do that. Best you have another rifle along."

The hick didn't disappoint.

"Okay, Captain," Tom said through freshly-licked lips. "Please tell Sheriff Creighton we're tracking the suspect. He'll be madder'n hell if we let his granddaughter's killer get away."

The boys filed past, heading to the left. Gerard motioned to Angelo and continued straight, on the main trail, until it finally ended. What had been nothing more than a defined rut, a wide path, an absence of vegetation and roots, simply became less. To the right, through a copse of mixed trees, sat a van, a tent, and a smoldering campfire—and Sheriff Creighton and his dog standing in front of two Gyps.

"Luca's not with them," Angelo whispered. "That's his sister. Conley claims she's psychic."

They watched and listened, hidden behind the furry boughs of a fat pine tree.

"The Sheriff will find Luca," Gerard said. "He's nobody's fool."

Angelo grunted. "And when he does, we'll be there to help."

Gerard nodded.

"My thoughts exactly."

****

"Luca Starbird—where is he?" Creighton said to the old man and the girl. She answered with a long, liquid stare, her body pressed tight against the old man hunched in a loose purple jacket, his face hidden under a fancy, wide-brimmed hat.

Leo the Traitor trotted to them, tail wagging. Hard to convey a sense of dread when your dog acted like the lead bitch of the Welcome Wagon.

The girl smiled and petted Leo. "What's his name, Sir?"

"His name is Leo. Where's Luca Starbird?"

Creighton didn't wait for an answer, but walked the perimeter of the site, studied the ground, and found footprints. He searched the tent and peered into the open side door of the van, his hand resting on the unicorn painting on the side panel. He knelt inside, a dank place redolent of staleness and sweat, moved a pile of clothes with the barrel of his gun, and lifted the mattress.

The girl was suddenly behind.

"You have no right in there, Officer."

"Move away."

"Luca isn't here," she insisted. "He's done nothing."

He lifted a sleeveless brown T-shirt and checked the tag—extra large. He balled it in his hand and climbed out. The girl was kneeling now, stroking Leo's mane, and the old man held a coffee cup with both hands. Steam rose from the ceramic mug, and its richness made Creighton's mouth water. A coffee pot sat on dying embers, with a spout curled like Aladdin's lamp. The aroma was intoxicating. He closed his eyes, and when he opened them they fixed on the old Gyp. Was this the ghost of his future? Still, relaxed, content, savoring a cup of joe. Loved and cared for by woman and dog. The life he longed for. The future a murderer had stolen.

He grabbed Leo's mane, yanked him roughly, and held the shirt under his nose. Leo looked at his master with inquisitive eyes and whimpered. Creighton squeezed his dog's fur and flesh. Leo sniffed the cloth and his demeanor suddenly changed. Tail rose, head straightened. Creighton followed him to an opening in the woods next to the van.

"Wait," the girl said and handed him a paper cup of coffee. "There's a chill in the air. Please accept our hospitality." The heat of the cup warmed Creighton's fingers and loosened them. The rich smell was irresistible. When he drank, the hot liquid burned his lips and the roof of his mouth, but slid down his throat like sweet custard.

The old man removed his hat and revealed a face that was a wrinkled map, a dark mask. His coffee cup was still full, he hadn't drank.

Creighton started away, but she caught his arm and he flinched. Her fingers had a strange, vibrant warmth, as if they were electrified.

"I know who you are," she said with a smile. Her eyes glistened. "I know you, Officer, and your beautiful wife. She says you've changed, she prays to have the man she knew back to help her through heartache. Finish your coffee, it'll help you. Then go to her and embrace your new life."

He unhooked his arm and squinted at the treetops. The clouds racing overhead looked full and bruised. The girl's silk shawl slid off her long hair. She held her open hand toward him and whispered. "Go to your wife. You're strong now. Don't let revenge consume you, not now, you're better than that."

He looked at the remaining coffee and poured it on the ground.

"No, I'm not," he said and followed his dog.

Chapter Twenty-Six

The dog pranced. The Sheriff shuffled.

Gerard and Angelo watched Creighton and the Gypsies from their hidden spot. The tableau of Gypsies, dog, and cop looked posed.

"Is he in the van?" Angelo asked.

"Patience," Gerard answered. "Our friend Creighton will lead us."

They waited, listening to Creighton's terse commands to the girl. The old man sat quiet. Suddenly, something was thrashing in the dense forest behind Angelo and Gerard.

"It's him," Angelo said. "He's running."

Angelo took off toward the sound and Gerard followed. A woodpecker started pecking. A crow added a caw. Angelo hurdled bushes and ran through thickets, and his pinwheeling arms made him look like a swimmer. At first, Gerard stayed close, but then he struggled to keep up even though Angelo had blazed the trail.

Light shone ahead in a clearing. Angelo shouted and drew his gun, and a man in the clearing turned and looked at him quizzically. Angelo squeezed the trigger and placed three bullets in the center of the wide chest. The crow cawed once, the man went down, and dry leaves billowed around him like dust.

Gerard caught up, wheezing, and ran to the fallen

man.

"Angelo!" Gerard shouted, eyes wide. "God! What did you do? Oh my God, it's not him! It's not Starbird!"

Angelo holstered his gun and drew the back of his hand across his mouth. The forest was quiet except for his tremulous voice.

"Then let's find him and get the hell out of here."

****

Creighton stopped at the sound of gunfire. Leo kept going, mewling his displeasure because he'd caught the Gypsy's scent. The right thing was for Creighton to see to his men—the shots had sounded small caliber, and the boys all had beefy weapons. Maybe some campers were just target shooting, but still...

It could wait. Leo begged with electric, pleading eyes, and Creighton followed his dog's brisk pace. Head down, he chose his footfalls and adjusted his peripheral vision, searching. As they strayed farther into the woods, the long grass, the bushes, the very dirt he tread on somehow became clearer and more vivid, as if his eyesight—in fact, all his senses—had sharpened. The broken underbrush threw off a woodsy fragrance, an invisible cloud of earthy smells.

But this sudden amplification of nature was having a strange effect on his hand. The fingers hadn't frozen again, even after the heat of the coffee cup subsided. In fact, they seemed stronger. For the first time he could remember, when he switched his gun to his bad hand, it felt as strong as his good.

Sounds got sharper, but not louder, and the woods darkened with shadow. Ahead, a high bluff hid the low sun. They traveled faster, sidestepping trees. The bottom of the cliff was in sight. Leo's body slunk in and out of the shadows. The cliff was a steep ascent, a sheer rock with sparse handholds and narrow crags. Did he see movement at the top? A face? Or simply branches swaying?

He put a hand on an outcrop and pulled himself up. Leo barked and he hushed him.

"Don't even start."

He climbed, and his arm felt strong, his body weightless. A giddiness came over him, a confidence. This high peak was a simple obstacle he'd make quick work of before confronting the murdering bastard.

Wind swooshed in his ear, the sun warmed his cheeks, and crevices seemed to magically appear every time he extended his hand. Soon he was halfway up and he suddenly hesitated. There was definitely movement above. *The Gypsy?* He extended from the rock and looked up at the face peering over the side. His breath stopped and his hands got clammy, for it wasn't Luca, but an impossible sight. The fair face of Dee-Dee looked down at him and spoke.

"Faster, Grandpa. Faster. Don't stop, you're almost here."

He pulled himself against the rock and shook his head. She'd seemed so real. Hadn't the body of his beloved Dee-Dee been laying under a blanket in that God-forsaken glen? Mike Harris had said it was his little girl and he'd never questioned it, even though the corpse on the ground was virtually unrecognizable.

The girl in the glen had been mutilated beyond recognition. *Maybe she was someone else.* He reached for the next hold and kicked up. Leo's barking was far away. Creighton was almost to the top.

Imagine how happy Janet will be.

No hold in sight now. The rock had solidified. Not a problem. The gap would open when his hand came close. He lifted with his feet, reached forward, and felt cold, slick hardness.

The sweet sound of his granddaughter's voice and the anticipation of Janet's surprise brought on the happiest feeling he'd ever experienced. His sweaty hand reached for the next crag, but he felt only smooth wall. When Creighton fell, separating slowly from the treacherous rock, he felt no alarm, no sense of dread, only a warm liquid wellspring of joy brought on by the physical vitality he'd found and the reincarnation of his beloved Dee-Dee.

Leo barked faster, louder.

Creighton imagined he'd finally caught his ride on a cloud, a comfortable cumulus whose puffs were as soft as snow. This elevator ride was all he ever dreamed it would be, cool air blowing through the bottom of the white cotton ball, and the rush soothing his aching back.

Leo's voice grew near. The treetops rushed by.

I saw her, Janet. I saw Dee-Dee. She's not dead at all.

****

Conley stood over the body of Patrick Runyan, half buried in leaves, his face in profile, eyes open in bewilderment. They'd separated earlier and traveled a wide circle around the sheriff's men. They'd known Luca would run, and had planned to head him off when he escaped the locals. Conley came running at the sound of the shot, for his intuition told him their plan had gone very wrong.

Now Runyan lay dead. His buckskin was soaked

with blood, his hands frozen into claws, as if he were carrying some invisible gift into the next world.

Campers had begun to stir. The sounds of voices and firewood being stacked carried through the trees. He sensed a presence and turned. The three Gypsies stood next to a gnarled oak. Gina approached and held her hand over Runyan's body. "You need to leave—before they come for you."

"I didn't kill him." He couldn't even believe he was saying the words.

"It doesn't matter. They'll blame us all. You should know that by now. You're an outsider like us."

Luca and the old man stood still and defiant. Gina stepped forward and took Conley's arm.

"Come. You're one of us now."

****

They traveled through the mountains overnight in the van, east to flat terrain. Luca drove and the old man slept except when coughing fits woke him. Blindly, Conley tried to process the catastrophe in the campground. His mind felt like it had snapped. How could everything go so wrong? A killer was on the loose, and it wasn't Luca Starbird.

Who killed Runyan? And for God's sake, *why*?

When they reached a seaside town in Maine called Harwell, a place the Gypsies seemed familiar with, they split up. Gina rented an apartment close enough to the bay to breathe air thick with the tang of salt water, while Luca took Pura elsewhere. In his mindless, rudderless state, it was all Conley could do to follow Lisa—no, Gina. The news said police blamed the Gypsies for Runyan's death, as Gina had predicted, and didn't mention that Conley was even in the vicinity.

Sheriff Creighton's climbing death was ruled accidental, but mysterious, and those words seemed to also serve as an apt description for the hunt for Alice and Dee-Dee's killer. Conley prayed the murders would be solved without his help.

For to help anyone seemed beyond him at the moment.

Seven months passed, the winter melted away, while Conley simply put one foot in front of the other each day and pretended to live a normal life in the peaceful town where they had landed. The feeling, the numbness, was oddly seductive. He even began to fantasize he'd somehow finally saved Luca, and the slate had been wiped clean. They were free, and no one was looking for them.

Meanwhile, his relationship with Gina blossomed into the affair he'd so guiltily craved since they first met.

Part 3

The Coast

Michael Walsh

Chapter Twenty-Seven

The front door to the only Catholic church in Harwell was smooth as glass. Should be. Officer Claire Lejeune and Father Remi Bourque had spent the weekend prior to Holy Week sanding it, until their fingers turned raw. They'd brought the oak back to its natural lightness, rubbing away a patina of salt, grime, and age. Then three coats of varnish, that was the ticket. The gloss made the grain pop, turning an ordinary portal into modern art.

But a smell like varnish had returned. Spray paint fouled the church's entrance, making it musty and dank. A pentagram had been painted on the door, and a swastika on the brick wall next to it. The outline of a phallus extended across St. Joe's marble nameplate. Vile. Heartbreaking.

Heartbreaking?

Just symbols, after all. Pictures. Words were hurtful arrows, but drawings, rough, jagged, imperfect sprays of paint with sloppy tendrils bleeding down? Were they sharper missiles? Apparently so. Satan probably had a quiver full of damned symbols.

"Father Bourque?" Claire said. "I'm so sorry."

She adjusted her uniform, a nervous tic she fought hard to lose. But her wide black belt, weighted with gun and handcuffs, pulled her pants, and the shirt was too tight across the chest.

"It's just paint, Claire. It'll come off and things will look good as new."

She followed him down the steep steps, and then they turned and took a last look at the façade from the sidewalk. Somehow the evil art seemed worse from afar, the lines less imperfect, the message more stark. They sat in the cruiser and shut the doors.

"We've got a few days until Easter, Claire. That's the good news. This is a very doable clean-up job. Scrub a little paint, that's all. God made the oceans in a day. We can knock out this chore."

She started the car and raised an eyebrow. "I admire your optimism, Father. Can't say I share it."

Their relationship was comfortable, their repartee that of old friends. Others sometimes tried to construe their closeness as something more, but it wasn't. Her job as a police officer often paired her with Father Bourque in the tiny burg of Harwell, that was all. His charm and innocence, strong will, and sterling character may have made him attractive to weaker women in the community, but not her. Professionals, especially those in law enforcement, couldn't afford to entertain fantasies. She turned her mind to business—and the crime at hand.

They drove down the long hill that was Armitage Street. The ferry idled near the bottom, nestled in its dock. Blue-black clouds stretched across the bay to Baker Island, trying hard to sully a pink sky. Stores were opening on either side of Armitage, canvas awnings ratcheting, tables and chairs being dragged to the front of the coffee shop. She smelled fresh butter croissants and her stomach rumbled.

Harwell residents, walking and working, greeted

one another, happy to be in a town small enough to know everyone. They passed the post office, library, bank, and the smiling faces of residents with a purpose-filled life. Parishioners, most of them—a faithful flock, these hard-working Mainers. Family and church, those were their passions, pursued in a cold but happy place. In no small way, Father Bourque was responsible. A good, handsome man with a pure heart and a wicked sense of humor—and a life dedicated to God. His optimism was often unfounded, a naiveté which somehow made him even more likable. She felt the need to rein him in.

"I still don't think this is a good idea, Father."

He lit a cigarette. A red pinpoint from the ember reflected in the windshield before him.

"Can't judge ideas until they're done, Claire. Their value's best seen in a rearview mirror."

She turned right on Spencer Street and traveled past gin mills and factories, onto the narrow canyon of Arthur Street, darkened by looming tenements on both sides. She parked and killed the engine.

"The Allen boy desecrated St. Joe's. There are witnesses. Jessie's a bad seed, always has been."

He snapped his cigarette into the gutter and looked at the building before him. Dew and shadow clung to the siding like wet gossamer. They climbed a creaking porch, entered through an unlocked door, and trudged up narrow, winding steps. They passed waist-high beadboard gouged and slashed, and plaster so grimy it looked like wallpaper. From a three-foot square landing they heard whimpering behind the wall of the second-floor apartment. They climbed to the third floor, the final landing. Bourque's breath was quick and labored.

He wiped his brow and breathed deep.

Claire knocked on the five-panel door. "You okay, Father? You're pale."

Inside, the sound of a television lowered to a murmur.

He smiled. "Altitude doesn't agree with me."

She knocked again. "Cigarette smoke doesn't agree with lungs, Father Bourque, just so you know." She grasped the knob and it turned freely. The corner of her mouth turned up.

"I think someone said, 'come in.'"

He shrugged. "Your hearing's better than mine."

Jessie Allen sat on the living room couch, arms folded, the sides of his loose sweatshirt bunched in his fists. Dark eyes, dark hair, arms and legs splayed at angles to his torso like a spider's. His feet were propped on a coffee table. Nothing moved except his head, which swiveled toward them on his tall, thin neck. His younger brother sat on the floor nearby, back against the couch, picture book open on his lap.

"You can't come in here," Jessie said.

Bourque jerked his thumb. "Officer Lejeune heard a cry for help."

"Our mother ain't home. She don't allow people in the apartment when she's workin'."

"We can come back later," Claire said. "We'll have a discussion with your mom about defacing St. Joe's, how's that sound?"

Clowns were running on the television screen, into a wooden building façade that began to fall. Music accentuated their pratfalls with drums and trumpets. The younger Allen closed his book and knelt straight, his head cocked like an attentive squirrel, his freckled face intent.

The stalemate continued. Jessie's cheeks hollowed. "What do you want here?" His voice had become low and guttural.

Bourque coughed and cleared his throat. "Glass of water would be nice."

The younger boy stood and walked to a kitchen area that was small and clean, and filled a glass. A green curtain skirt stretched across the base of the porcelain sink. Three chairs surrounded a small table. "You have a nice brother, Jessie. He has good manners." The boy handed him the water. "I brought something for you two."

He eyed Bourque's hands, then Claire's. "What did you bring?"

"They brought nothing," Jessie said. "They're liars, Tommy, talking heads. He lies in church and she lies every time her lips move."

Tommy sat back on the floor. Claire wrung her hands and pressed her lips tight.

Bourque took a long drink. "Opportunity, Tommy. That's what I brought."

Jessie's voice was sharp. "See? He's not giving us anything. Liar, just like I said."

Heat bloomed in Claire's cheeks. She stepped forward and her words practically exploded. "Watch your mouth."

"Listen," Bourque said. "I want to give you a chance to restore a beautiful place, a rarer opportunity than you think. I need help cleaning St. Joe's."

"I didn't do nothing at the front of that church," Jessie said, "and you can't prove otherwise."

"I didn't say you did. And I didn't mention the

front of the church. Besides, I'm talking to your brother right now. It'd be a pleasure working with you, Tommy."

Jessie answered. "Work ain't pleasure and he ain't interested."

Claire couldn't contain herself. "The town jail ain't pleasure either, you punk."

Bourque stepped in front of her. "Help me clean the church and I promise you'll never regret it. You boys are too young to know regret, but believe me, it's an unpleasant companion."

"Time for you to leave," Jessie said.

"Not every day you get to erase a mistake with a little elbow grease, and then admire your handiwork. People will compliment you, you'll be proud, and God will smile a little brighter."

"Shut up." Jessie rose, tall and gangly, his baggy shirt spread wide. "Shut up."

Bourque looked at the ceiling. "I'll get to walk out of the rectory every morning and see the sun bounce off the brick again, see the brightwork shine on the doors, and the gold letters glitter in the marble masthead. People will walk by and say what a good job we did. It's a real thrill, Tommy—better than a hundred dollars in your pocket."

Jessie again. "We ain't stupid. This is a trick to get me to admit something I didn't do."

"No, not at all. This is forgiveness, pure and simple. Officer Lejeune and I made a deal. Just help clean. Or not. Either way, she's agreed to forget the whole incident."

"Why?"

"So you'll help for the right reason."

The music on the television stopped. The clowns were standing still. Jessie unfolded his arms and legs. His tight jaw and hard eyes softened and his hand extended—slightly. Tommy looked at his brother. Bourque held out his hand and Claire prayed it would be accepted. *Make this scheme work, light a path for Jessie Allen.*

Claire regretted her earlier words—*I admire your optimism. Can't say I share it.*

Faith, not optimism, Claire, Father Bourque had answered. *Admire my faith.*

Dear Lord, allow this humble servant to rescue a soul from the edge of darkness—just this once. Come on, Jessie. Take his hand.

Suddenly Jessie Allen's hand drew back and closed to a fist.

"You got a dirty church and that's your problem. Tell God to wipe it away." He stepped to the television, kicked his brother's book on the way, and turned up the volume. Music again, a loud instrumental, staccato. Tommy's eyes stayed on Bourque.

"Tommy," Bourque yelled over the blare. "You come. Help us clean the church."

"Bitch and bastard," Jessie screamed. "Get out, bitch and bastard." His voice thundered.

The floor started to clap, a loud, sharp knocking that added to the din, a protest from the neighbor below.

Claire withdrew. Her uniform suddenly felt slack and baggy, as if she had shrunk inside it. Her voice sounded small. "You are stupid, Jessie."

"Let's go, Claire." Father Bourque grasped her trembling forearm.

She pulled away. "No, Father, we can't let this be."

"Claire."

Tommy was still as stone. Bourque pulled Claire out the door and when it closed behind them the shouting and squawk of the TV muted. Descending the stairs, she spoke to his back.

"Satisfied, Father? The idea's done now. Satisfied? We accomplished nothing and their lives are unraveling."

"Or maybe unfolding, Claire."

She shook her head. "Sometimes I think we speak different languages. Why did I agree to this? I should've arrested Jessie and let him fry in the pokey for a day."

They clopped down the stairs, their palms flat against the filthy wall for support. Outside, she walked around the car before looking back. Her companion had not moved from the bottom of the steps. She imagined he was crestfallen in his failure. She felt a compassionate urge to hug him, to stroke her hand down his back, and tell him it wasn't his fault. Saving humanity was not a job for humans.

"You worry me, Father."

He grinned. "You sound like my mother."

He eyed the front door of the falling porch, the peeling paint, the grimy window, and the yellowed shade.

"We'd better get started," she said before she sighed and considered Father Bourque.

Was this really his calling, his mission? Another failure to be added to a long list of failures—add the unsuccessful rescue of the reprobate Allen boys from delinquency to countless nights spent counseling couples who always seemed to ultimately divorce, and to many days spent preaching to drunks who rifled the poor box after AA meetings in the church basement. She lamented another of his failures, even though he always seemed to take them in stride.

His words brought her back from her reverie.

"Just a minute, Claire." His chin lifted and his eyes drifted toward the door.

Did it move? She'd seen something too, and wondered whether God had taken mercy on His faithful servant and reconsidered. Father froze and waited, his patrician profile full of hope and faith. She dreaded his disappointment.

"Father," she called, "you can't save everyone."

The door opened wider and Tommy appeared on the threshold, working his arms into his jacket. His long hair curled out from under a ball cap. Hand on the knob, one foot out the door, he suddenly turned to look at something behind in the hallway, something that cast a shadow—a large shadow that darkened his red hair and shaded his fair face.

Jessie Allen's spider-like arm shot forward, snatched his brother's hand, and pulled him back up the stairs.

Chapter Twenty-Eight

Alarm.

The tin clock chattered across the night table in Conley and Gina's Harwell apartment on a cold March morning. Such a cruel way to end sweet dreams. Conley shut the alarm, turned, and caressed Gina's shoulder. The threadbare cotton sheets, worn to a silky comfort, tightened and slid across their bare skin as if oiled. Reluctantly, he swung his bare feet onto the cold floor and pulled on his jeans and boots. He quietly closed the bedroom door and turned on the kitchen light. The fluorescent flickered in the kitchen and made the rust in the porcelain sink sparkle like flecks of gold.

He poured cereal and milk into a bowl, and sat at the table. The cereal had begun to stale, the milk had begun to sour. Water dripped from the kitchen faucet insistently, the wall clock ticked, and the introspection and regret that visited during early, quiet mornings returned. The choice he'd made to join the Gypsies seemed insane now, the impulsive decision to abandon his career and his life in Ocean Park. He'd told himself he had to protect the innocent—Luca—from a vigilante rush to judgment, but doubts nagged. Had he simply abandoned his duty because he couldn't cope with the death of Lisa, the hunt for Alice and Dee-Dee's killer, and the frustration of being powerless against the growing carnage?

The Devil whispered Gina's warm flesh was the real reason.

Didn't matter. He was protecting her brother, as promised. No one was looking for Luca, in fact Conley wasn't even sure where he and Pura were. Somewhere on the island across the channel.

The refrigerator growled to life. Water suddenly whooshed through the pipes in the wall.

Gina pattered into the kitchen in her nightgown, hugged him, and nuzzled his neck. He wondered if she'd read his thoughts, and he scolded himself for the unfounded suspicion. She whispered the name she'd given him—Jack. Answering to another's name was oddly comforting, almost as comforting as the arrival of an old friend he thought was gone forever. In this bizarre new life, he welcomed a visitor called *Peace*.

****

Later that day, a bulky sofa fought Conley. Its rolled leather arms were impossible to grip and the flared back seemed to have no purpose except to prevent it from passing through the mansion's front doorway. He and Mullen struggled, turning it several ways, until his fingers ached and his forearms felt hard as stone.

"Think, Jack," Mullen said. "Turn it another way. Use your brain." Mullen's brown eyes burned, the flat planes of his angular face tightened, and the cords in his neck pulsed and gave life to the tattoo flames rising from under his collar.

Conley looked behind. Shawn and Hawk came out of the back of the moving truck and their boots clanked on the inclined metal ramp.

"You're hurtin' the cause, Jack," Mullen muttered.

"Turn the fucker."

Conley tried to better his grip. Sweat rolled down his arms. The couch end slid through his slicked hands and its wood feet clapped the oak floor.

Mullen dropped his corner, stabbed his finger in the air, and backpedalled into the house. "I ain't working with him, Shawn. You teach him, he's useless."

Shawn and Hawk stood beside Conley, studying the doorway. They squatted at either end of the sofa and lifted. Shawn inched backward in measured steps and Hawk did the same moving forward. They quietly turned the couch and angled it with precision. Within seconds the leather was gleaming in the sunshine.

"Don't sweat it, Jackie," Shawn said and clapped Conley's shoulders. "You'll get so you can eyeball monsters like this one." The tips of his red hair were dark with sweat, his pale face flush with exertion. "It's a mind game, that's all. Just picture the thing floating out the door."

They carried it toward the truck, legs moving in sync, and suddenly stopped. Shawn nodded toward the house.

"Kid's touchy, Jack. Apologize to him, will ya? Tell him I'll buy him a beer, cool him off."

Conley stepped back inside, through the foyer, into the great room. Tall windows overlooked the beach and ocean. Dunes stretched to crashing waves. The room looked cavernous without furniture and curtains. He called to Mullen and the name echoed. Surly punks like Mullen used to straighten their backs and widen their eyes at the sight of him and Angelo. And even if that tribute was only because of the fear of a tin badge, it wasn't any less satisfying. Respect was a narcotic every cop craved.

He searched every room, his footsteps echoing. The kitchen looked like a silver-plated and brown-granite factory, the study a rich mahogany tomb with empty shelves dusted with white. He climbed the winding staircase. The window view changed from blue ocean and white foam to blue sky and white clouds.

He lowered the brass handle and opened the door to the master bedroom. Mullen turned to him quickly, his thin face reflected three times in the tri-fold mirror on a woman's built-in dresser. Six eyes glared, dark and piercing. A jewelry chest sat in the mirror nook, antique white with gold knobs, evidently forgotten by the owners. The top knob was out of line with the others because a drawer was pulled forward. The white knuckles of Mullen's fists rested on the dresser, and Conley saw his own reflection in the mirror between the columns of Mullen's straightened arms.

The surf outside thundered. Sunlight streamed through the windows. Mullen simply stared, the prismed beams of light washing over his face. He lifted his chin.

"What the fuck you lookin' at?"

Ask about the open drawer. Ask if the bulges in the kid's pockets were something he'd care to explain.

But the Mullens of the world, their actions, were a worry of the past. Those things didn't matter to *Jack.* They'd been burned away by the light of a new, shimmering day.

Conley bared his teeth and smiled, and was surprised at the calmness in his voice.

"Sorry I screwed up with the couch, bro. Let's get

out of here. Shawn wants to buy us a beer."

****

They sat at a table near the bar and ordered beer. A jukebox blared, which didn't stop Shawn from jabbering nonstop. Hawk lifted a bottle and drained it—three swallows and done.

Mullen stood, carried his bottle to the bar, and leaned close to a young woman sitting on a stool. She smoothed her long blond hair and smiled.

"Your knees sore, Jackie?" Shawn shouted over the noise. "Ice 'em. That's important, right, Hawk? That's your best bet."

Hawk ignored him and raised four fingers to the barmaid.

"Hawk and me been moving so long we don't even feel our muscles anymore. Pain's in the brain, that's all."

The girl at the bar was giggling and leaning her shoulder into Mullen's chest.

"Mullen's discovered Lily," Shawn said and grinned. "The town punch. Bitch got more diseases than the dictionary."

Lily was still smiling, eyes sparkling, teeth gleaming. She lifted her glass with a bent hand, drank, and giggled some more.

"She likes to play coy," Shawn said. "Pretends she don't want it." He laughed and beer dribbled from his mouth.

Lily slipped off the stool and fell against Mullen, her hands on his hips. His nostrils flared and his hand drifted down and over her ass. She didn't object.

The jukebox song changed and the bar crowd got louder. Shawn lowered his head.

"Drink up, boys." He touched the neck of his beer to Conley's and Hawk's. His glassy eyes shone. "Here's to loose women and hard men."

****

The bar was still buzzing with laughter and music when they left. They walked to Shawn's car in the back of the crowded lot, through a cloud created by their frosted breath. Conley turned his collar up and dug his hands deeper in his pockets.

The inside of Shawn's car was illuminated by faint moonlight and a lit cigarette. Mullen and Lily were in the darkened back seat, the ember of her cigarette dancing like a firefly before she threw it out the window.

The three of them turned away and waited. Was Alice Starke romanced like this before she died? Were her eyes expressive, bright, filled with the promise of passion like Lily's had been in the bar? Did Deidre Creighton smoke a cigarette, her hand moving in the same arcs?

And was their killer like Mullen?—charming, funny—evil?

Shawn shifted from one foot to the other. Hawk's head was tilted toward the sky, his eyes still covered by sunglasses reflecting the moon.

The car shuddered again and a muffled scream followed. They were fighting.

Was this how Alice and Deidre had struggled?

What happened when passion turned to terror?

Did their eyes widen? Did their cries excite the killer?

Another scream.

Shawn and Hawk started toward the car. Conley

ran past, his feet sliding in the gravel. He unlatched the door and threw it open. The dome light bleached the pair's shirtless torsos. Mullen's dark tattoo rippled on his heaving chest. Lily was a study in contrasts—pale skin flecked with blood from her swollen lips. She darted past, and Mullen tumbled out and attacked Conley with lazy jabs and slow roundhouses. Conley fought back hard and soon had Mullen backward on the hood of the car.

Strong hands circled Conley's biceps. Shawn and Hawk pinned him on the ground.

"Surprise, surprise. Our friend Jackie has mettle," Conley heard Shawn mutter. "Just the type of mettle we're looking for."

Chapter Twenty-Nine

The Harwell ferry to Baker Island was the victim of a sloppy mooring. Gina felt woozy on her Wednesday trip to Pura and Luca because the *Casco Lady* was swaying like a drunkard and knocking the pier so hard the pilings shook. The ship's condition was appalling. Its peeling wheelhouse needed a paint job, and its hull was gouged and scarred with black slashes that looked like war paint. It slammed against tires nailed to the pier, squeezing the bumpers so hard they blatted like flatulence. Captain McCloud turned to an old woman nearby.

"Have a seat, Mrs. Dumars. We're about to launch."

"When I'm good and ready, Mr. McCloud. I am a paying passenger, you know. You were politer before you took my fare."

"Please take a seat, Mrs. Dumars. Maritime law."

"Don't hide behind laws, Mr. McCloud. It's demeaning."

She raised a hand to end the conversation.

A drunk lolled in the back. A couple bickered loudly. Gulls circled the bow, drawn by bread crumbs that children were throwing over the side.

"Enough, children," the old woman said, still on the move. "Those birds are scavengers, you know. They carry all sorts of disease and they soil those who feed them." She lifted an eyebrow at the parents sitting behind and muttered, "Bad manners are the spoiled fruit of poor upbringing."

Another woman called hello and tried to keep pace, a difficult task because she had a limp and shuffle. Her dark coat was covered with lint and a heavy broach hung over her heart.

"Florence Dumars, you're looking lovely this morning. I saved our seats. Over here, where you like it. Away from the salt spray and wind."

They sat near Gina, and because they were upwind she could hear every word. She pushed more of her hair under her kerchief and closed her coat tighter. The one called Florence spoke to her pleasant companion, her steely eyes fixed on Gina.

"Look at the girl with the hoop in her ear and the bandana, Ella."

"Maybe she's metis."

Metis. Gina knew what that meant—mixed blood, Indian and white, and though it wasn't true, she recognized the prejudice and hate for an outsider all too well.

"She's probably just a potato picker," Ella continued, smiling and waving three fingers.

Gina adjusted the drawstring bag she carried over her shoulder like the migrants did, full and buttoned, and laid her paisley handbag on the seat next to her. McCloud's crew unhooked the ship's lines. The Captain blew his horn and they set off for Baker Island. The ocean wove under them like ribbons, the ship's oily discharge mixing with dark currents.

Ella had a question. "Are you comfortable, Florence? I know you like it, but this isn't the best place to sit, you know."

"Shhh. Just listen to me, don't interrupt. That girl's no potato picker, Ella, not by a long shot. Have you seen her before?"

"Before what?"

"Ever. Ever. Have you ever seen her?"

Ella looked up and used her hands to shield the sun. "I don't think I've seen her. Ever, I mean. Why?"

Florence turned toward Baker Island, a half mile away, her face tight in concentration. Gina rummaged in her handbag and re-arranged the contents. Something was afoot.

"I like her bag, Flo."

"Pay attention, Ella. We dock soon. Stay close, and no more of your shuffling. Be quick and be ready. We'll follow at a distance and track the courier—"

"Courier of what, Flo? What's she carrying?"

"Just do what you're told."

"But what if she sees us?"

"Once we determine her destination, I'll stay and you'll fetch the constable."

"But why, Flo? What has she done? What will we tell him?"

The *Casco Lady* slowed. The bow dug into still water and the stern rose on the crest of the boat's wake. The entrance to the tiny harbor was just ahead. Passengers on the island pier stood at attention, eyes right, watching the entrance.

"You'll tell him Florence Dumars has saved his backward little island from the perils of civilization, that's what. Drugs, or some other contraband, maybe worse. Tell him his deputies were napping while crime made headway."

The horn blew. The ship slowed to a crawl and broadsided the pier with a sickening crunch. Those waiting to board lurched backward. McCloud's men jumped to the cleats with coils of line. Passengers on the ferry stood and queued to the exit. Florence waited for Gina to go and stayed a discreet distance behind. Ella followed like static electricity. Gina hurried through the crowd, turning sideways to get by.

"We're losing her. Hurry," was the last thing she heard Florence say.

Gina was nearing the gangplank. She looked back. Ella stood sideways in the aisle, one bony arm raised, the other pointing at the bench where Gina had sat—and deliberately left the paisley handbag behind. Florence hesitated before making a beeline to the bench. She snatched the bag and fumbled with the metal clasp. The ferry had emptied and oncoming passengers were being held at the bottom of the gangplank by Captain McCloud.

"Mrs. Dumars," she heard him call. "Mrs. Roy, passengers are waiting. Please disembark."

Florence struggled to open the clasp. Suddenly she looked up and ripped the broach from Ella's lapel. Her hand flew to the new tear in her coat. When Florence fit Ella's beloved piece under the metal clasp, stones popped from the breastpin and fell on the wide planks. The bag finally opened.

New passengers were boarding. "Really, Mrs. Dumars," Captain McCloud pleaded. His stout face was red and his eyes burned.

Florence Dumars turned the bag upside down and the flap swung open. Its contents appeared lodged, stuck. Finally The Book, with its gilt edges and gold-embossed cross, shook loose on its own, tumbled in the air, and bounced off Florence's toe. The Bible cartwheeled away, four corners drumming the weathered deck until finally coming to rest spine-down, its open pages fluttering in the breeze.

****

The ferry horn blew behind her. Gina passed the general store, island post office, and gingerbread houses painted in rainbow colors. She crossed a bridge that spanned an inlet from ocean to marsh, and turned onto a narrow trail between high weeds. She climbed a rocky hill and traversed a meadow onto a plateau of long grass and ragweed. The trek to the leeward side of the island, to its high cliffs and crashing waves, always seemed longer than she remembered. The fishing shack she sought sat on one cliff and under another. Its weathered siding blended into the pewter sky and gray rock. Smoke rose from the chimney.

She opened the door. Pura was alone, sleeping on a cot in the corner of the tiny shack. The walls shivered from the wind. Windows rattled. The place was as dank and cold as a cave. She knelt next to him. His hands were warm, pulse strong, and his face was burning. She retrieved a bottle from her string sack, wet her fingers, and ran them across his parched lips. Pura's skin had softened. His face used to be wrinkled. Now the crow's feet were barely discernible, the laugh lines smooth. The creases in his brow had become shadows.

"He has fever again." Luca was suddenly next to her, kneeling, his breath warming her cheek.

"Then he needs to drink. He needs to sleep." She retrieved a salt cube from the sack and ran it across Pura's newly-wet lips.

"His spirit is sick," Luca said. "He needs to return to his family. Kumpania."

"It's not safe," she said.

"When has it ever been?"

The hair on Luca's temples had started to lighten and gray. His face was tighter, the jawbone defined.

"It's not safe," she repeated.

"Ahh, your *gadjo* tells you so. Your beloved *gadjo*."

"No, he doesn't, Luca. I feel it. Me."

"You feel? You used to see, Gina." He touched her arm. "But you don't see the future anymore, do you? Just the past. You've lost part of the gift God gave you. What's that tell you, sister?"

Pura opened his soft, liquid eyes. She smiled at him, wiped his face with a wet cloth, turned to her brother, and pushed his hand away.

"It tells me I no longer have to see the judgment God has planned, Luca. And that's the greatest blessing of all."

Chapter Thirty

Old brick buildings cast cool shadows on Conley and Gina as they stopped in front of a downtown store window on Saturday afternoon, and she locked her arm in his.

"Beautiful," she said.

They stared at a mannequin, impossibly thin, with a pale, angular face that looked alien. A red blouse hung from its torso and tight jeans hugged its rounded hips. The plaster hands were outstretched in a gesture of bewilderment, an expression reinforced by its wide eyes and arched eyebrows.

"Let's take a look," he said.

"I already know. They're too expensive."

He kissed the top of her head. "Not to try them on."

Inside, two matrons led her to the dressing room. He sat in a hard chair, opened his wallet, and counted the bills—less bills than he thought, and he suddenly remembered the subject of money was one of Angelo's favorite rants.

Women want money, Conley. We lust for them and they lust for a fat wallet.

He tried to forget—channeling Angelo was never healthy. Besides, Gina wasn't so shallow she'd lust for a pretty blouse and stylish jeans—or was she? The truth was he didn't really know. Talk about shallow, he'd fallen like a schoolboy for her, and as with all purely physical attractions, his knowledge of her was only skin deep.

Power and money, that's what broads want. Angelo's miserable practicality again. His pessimism was contagious.

Gina came out of the dressing room and stood on the platform in front of a three-fold mirror. The jeans fit her lithe body like a second skin. Three reflections of Gina shone, two profiles and a straight-on image. He froze. The overhead light made her black hair shine.

Black. But Lisa's hair was red.

She pressed her hand to her waist, smoothed the pants over her thighs and the sleeves over her arms. His head began to ache, and when he looked up he saw his own weary, ashen face in the mirror.

Love? Love's a chimera, Conley. You know what that means? No? Well, look it up.

She frowned at him and turned the tag.

"They're a lot of money," she said. "Do you really like them?"

A matron pecked her head toward him and raised her eyebrows. "Beauty has no price," she offered.

"Neither does love," the other one chimed.

Gina let go of the tag and walked back to the changing room. The matron winked at him.

Money or power, Conley. Money or power. The voice was insistent.

She came back again, in a skirt this time, and when she stepped to the mirror, Conley couldn't stop staring at her olive-colored legs, her beautiful dark features, her perfect smoothness. Gina raised up on her tiptoes, muscles taut, and gazed at her synchronized preening images.

Beautiful—but foreign, unlike any he'd ever seen.
Unlike Lisa's.

When she left for the dressing room he cradled his face in his hands. His obsession with Gina was born from her resemblance to Lisa, but that twin had disappeared, replaced by a stranger he didn't know. He felt like he'd just woken with the mother of all hangovers.

Third time—she wore a matching suit, a professional-looking outfit, and the way she moved and turned, with the lean body of an athlete or a dancer, was like nothing he'd ever seen.

She was gorgeous, a dark beauty—*and a total stranger*. She left once more, and on her way by she frowned at his image in the mirror, and he soon knew why. He looked like he'd lost his soul.

Chapter Thirty-One

The lines in Shawn's palms were deep and dark, and they bisected pads of muscled flesh and stretched to knuckles as big as quarters. His hand reached into his shirt pocket, delicately pinching a piece of paper, and he drew it out, his smooth, blunt fingertips carving the air when he spoke. He sounded conciliatory, as if apologizing for the hands, over which he had no control.

"Sorry to ruin your Monday, Mr. Lewis, but we got a problem."

The check he held was pale yellow, its lettering gold. The flowing black script contrasted nicely. The red letters that angled across did not.

INSUFFICIENT FUNDS

Lewis read. He unbuttoned the left cuff of his white safari shirt with his right hand and rolled the sleeves. His fingers were slim and nimble—piano players—and the black hair on his forearms rose slowly when the sleeve rolled back. He glanced over his shoulder. Mrs. Lewis was lifting china from a box on the dining room table and arranging pieces in a hutch. She slowed and looked to the doorway as her husband worked the other arm.

"Gotta be some kind of screw-up," he said. Both sleeves were rolled tight and squeezing his biceps. "Bring it back to your bank and tell 'em to run it again."

Shawn smiled and waved the check.

"I got no use for banks, Mr. Lewis. But my wife works for this one, and she usually ain't wrong."

Mrs. Lewis padded in bare feet to her husband and stood behind him. Her right arm circled his waist, her left hand rested on his shoulder. Sunlight made her diamond ring white, as pale as her hand.

"Problem, honey?"

"Workmen got an issue."

Hi, Mrs. Lewis," Shawn said. "Remember us? We're the movers. We thought Mr. Lewis and Jackie and me could take a drive down to the bank and sort this out."

Lewis laughed.

"No, boys. That ain't gonna happen. Don't bother my wife with this shit. Learn to listen. You two are going to get in your truck and drive to the bank, understand?" He rolled his eyes and searched the air over their heads. "I don't have time for this."

Shawn returned the check to his pocket. The neighborhood sounds grew quiet. Birds quit singing. A lawnmower coughed to a stop. The street was empty.

"Make time."

Mrs. Lewis' ring hand tightened. Her husband's chin lifted, as if he'd suddenly decided to pose in the doorframe. He whispered in her ear. Her hands retracted and she disappeared into another room. He bared his teeth and his eyes met Shawn's. "Fuck off." He swung the door shut and the latch clicked sharply.

Shawn studied the gleaming six-panel door, raised his arm, and pounded with the underside of his fist. The rough texture of his leathery hand was as defined as the grains in the oak door.

Conley said, "Shawn, let it go."

The hand stopped and rested on the wood. The voices of the Lewises—arguing—were muffled by the expensive door, the brick walls, the storm windows.

Conley laid his hand on Shawn's rock-hard forearm.

"Not here, not now. Just let it go."

****

Later that day, Shawn's cellar door opened on creaky hinges. Number two heating oil tinged the air. A curved ceiling angled sharply down, and the steps that led to the cellar were dark and worn. Unpainted drywall lined both sides, and his and Conley's footsteps loosened bits of joint compound that tumbled down the stairs ahead of them.

Movie posters, wrinkled and crooked, hung on the basement's concrete walls. Mismatched scatter rugs covered the floor, and toys sat neatly in a corner. Footsteps scurried overhead—children—and Shawn's wife Mary working in the kitchen.

Conley and Shawn crossed a playroom, passed through an open balsa-wood door, and entered a dark paneled office consisting of a clean desk, two plain chairs, and a gray five-drawer file. The panels held plaques, awards, a painting of sailboats in a harbor. A photo of a young, crew-cut Shawn and his father hung in a frame. Shawn sat behind the desk and opened a drawer.

"Take a load off, Jackie. Don't mind the ruckus upstairs. Mary lost her job at the bank today and she's in a pissy mood. One day they have her running the whole works, the next day she's excess overhead."

Upstairs, water splashed in the kitchen sink. Pots and pans scraped. The children were whining and complaining. Mary snapped at them. The kids started crying, and the sound seemed amplified as it drifted through the perforated ceiling tiles.

Shawn pulled a check register out of a desk drawer and opened the cover. "You doing okay, Jackie?"

No, Shawn, I'm almost broke. Rent's due, refrigerator's empty, and the power company's threatening to turn the heat off. No, I'm certainly not okay—but you've got enough on your plate.

"Sure. Listen, I can ride for a week or two. I started tending bar a couple nights a week down at Cronin's. You don't have to pay me today."

He kept writing, head down, tore the check on its perforation, and held it to Conley.

"Then I'd be a deadbeat, Jackie. Then I'd be Lewis."

Conley folded the check and slid it into his shirt pocket.

Suddenly all was quiet upstairs, no more footsteps, no more clanging pots and pans, no more crying.

Shawn looked up. "The kids have been sick. Mary took time off to take care of them. Too much time, evidently. Probably the real reason the bank let her go."

"I'm sorry, Shawn. I was thinking maybe you should file a complaint about Lewis with the police. Don't let him get away with this."

"No, I done that before. Lots of paperwork and nothing ever to show for it in the end. Listen, you and me gotta talk, Jackie."

Shawn sat back and folded his arms. He locked his icy blue eyes on Conley's.

"I heard some things, serious stuff. I heard there's trouble in your past. But I don't care. I think maybe it's all noise. Like hearsay, y'know? My gut tells me you're stand-up."

"What are you saying, Shawn?"

"I'm saying I know about you, Matt Conley, that's what."

While Matt's stomach sank, Shawn opened a file cabinet drawer and it squealed on the track. "So let's cut the bullshit. Remember what I said to Lewis about banks? I hate banks, Jackie! Banks are symbols. Symbols of greed. A sign of all that's wrong in this man's world. They exist on the backs of working stiffs like us. Like you and me—right?"

Conley's throat went dry. He was screwed. What was Shawn planning with his newfound information? Blackmail? A reward?

"Sure," Conley said, preparing for the worst, preparing for the next steps in his crumbling life. More running, lying, hiding? A weariness enveloped him. "Whatever. Sure, I hate banks, too."

Shawn retrieved a roll of paper and spread it on the desk—a blueprint, a crisp white sketch of a building on a powder-blue background. Windows and doors were circled in pencil, measurements underlined. Notes in black ink lined the edges. A portion of the roof was highlighted with yellow marker.

Footsteps tapped on the cellar stairs. Mary descended them slowly, deliberately, arms folded, and sat next to her husband. He stood, hair hanging over his eyes, his hands spread flat on the edges of the print, arms locked. His face was as dark as clay. Block letters—*CASCO NATIONAL BANK*—stretched across the bottom of the page. His lips barely moved when he spoke.

"How much do you hate them, Detective Matt Conley?"

Chapter Thirty-Two

The old library complained. Floorboards creaked under the tap of the librarian's footsteps, peeling Palladian windows shuddered in the wind, and cast iron radiators whistled. On Wednesday, Conley sat on a hard chair and signed on to the *Ocean Park Gazette's* website. The masthead of last week's *Gazette* flashed onto the screen, with flowing Gothic font and today's date—April 1. The winter, interminably long, had drawn out like a blade until finally the last snow melted and the breeze off Casco Bay carried a hint of warmth.

But nothing had changed.

The chair was hard and the table wobbled. The dust on the back of the old desktop computer burned into a swill-like stench. The key to proving Luca Starbird's innocence hid in the screen in front of him, of that he was sure, and the conviction gnawed like a splinter under his skin.

He opened his spiral notebook and searched the newspaper's archives. Every front page had shouted *Alice Starke* during the first weeks after her death. News stories flashed across the dusty screen, black print on a white background sullied with a nicotine tint.

The librarian walked by, a stack of books cradled in her arm. Thick-lensed glasses magnified her eyes.

Back to the screen, to a quote and a moment he remembered. "Never seen anythin' like it," an Ocean

Park cop said to a reporter as they stood over Alice's body and a breeze rippled the blanket that covered her. "The sticks in her eyes, I mean. They were the same gray as her face."

Another click of the mouse, and more text to mine. The print was small, and he experimented with enlarging the display. He pinched his nose, blinked, and continued.

Angelo's name appeared often. The reports were information Conley already knew, but he had to read them all again because enlightenment might shine from innocent quotes and innocuous observations, from nouns and verbs. He wrote when he saw a glimmer, and the written pages grew.

Grew toward what? A revelation, some brainchild? Or a delusion? Didn't matter. Just read, read, read, and write, and hope the dead speak from the printed page.

Click.

Fewer headlines about Alice. Political elections and fall harvest festivals had pushed her to the back pages. Angelo claimed to know why.

People forget, Conley. Remember, people forget.

Click.

To a photo of him and Angelo, heads bent toward the ground—*contemplating a clue or simply tired?* Angelo's caustic voice rose from the picture.

People forget, Conley.

He switched to the *Northcountry News*, to another name—Deidre Creighton. The coverage was crude and bizarre. The story was too big for volunteer students and bored matrons dabbling with journalism. They interviewed locals, as if reporting rape and mutilation warranted the same tactic as town meetings and 4-H contests.

"Girl thought she was sophisticated," her next-door neighbor said.

What's that mean?

"She took chances," Deidre's mailman offered.

Ahh—small-town speak for Wild.

Click, click. He was woozy again, nauseous. The librarian was suddenly behind, leaning over his shoulder, her person redolent of bubble gum, perfume, and musty books. "Everything all right, Mr. Smith?"

"Yes. Thanks. A little vertigo, that's all."

"Too much reading on a computer will do that." Her hands cupped his shoulders. "Head librarian calls it See Sickness. The cure is to look away for a while. Do something else."

He closed his eyes and breathed deep. When he opened them she was gone.

Good advice. He turned away from the computer to his notebook.

Deidre. Dee-Dee. A girl with dangerous beauty and an undeniable edge. A few too many boyfriends, an itch too big for a backwoods burg.

But what was she really like? What color was her world? He turned a page and took a crack at story-telling. Why not?

Dee-Dee swung her legs over the side of the bed and stretched. Snow was collecting on the bottom of her bedroom window, filling the air outside, building a white blanket on pine needles. Today was special, today was skating day. Snow covered the pond near the river, and she and her friends would skate patterns in the powder, circles and hearts, and fill them with snow angels.

She walked barefoot across the floor, the shag rug tickling her feet. Into the closet, in search of her favorite skating skirt. Grandpa had just lined the walls with cedar and now her closet smelled delicious, like freshly-cut trees. In fact, she named it the outside-in room, and that made her grandmother laugh...

Words flowed. The pen had moved on its own. Pages filled. His head was clear now.

Let's try it with Alice.

She fished for lipstick in the nightstand drawer. Color didn't matter, as long as her lips looked defined and full. She'd been to one dance already, and the dim lights made girls look plain and gray. She studied her face in the hand mirror, twisted the lipstick tube, and applied more. Hard to concentrate, listening to her father's demented laughter, the TV's laugh track, the drone of eighteen-wheelers screaming down the interstate in her backyard. Their wash made the tin trailer shake and howl like a wind tunnel. Swoo-o-o-sh.

Best to ignore those sounds and enjoy the rainbow lights, the colored squares her new mirror ball sprinkled from the ceiling. And when the first boy asked her to dance, she'd pretend the darkness in the gym was speckled with a thousand lights, just like her bedroom, and they'd kiss...

He created more pages. Getting the hang of it— painting pictures with ink and cursive script.

So what? To what end, writing these stories? A waste of time. Creating stories about the dead felt like sacrilege. Let them sleep.

But they don't seem to want to.

He turned to a new page and touched the ballpoint to the first line. The pen worked so fast the shaft trembled. The words poured onto the page.

The librarian placed a cup of water on the rocking table and slipped away. He watched her as she walked away.

Thank you, Big Eyes, for opening mine.

****

Gina shrugged into her coat on Saturday evening. She placed the long drawstring bag on the kitchen chair and untied it. The last ferry would leave in an hour and Pura needed medicine. She checked the bag again, read the drug store bottle, twisted the cap, and eyed the pills. Baker Island was too far away to travel and forget something.

Drawers slid closed in the bedroom and the closet door creaked open. Conley's boots pecked across the floor. Water from the bathroom faucet splashed in the sink.

His notebook lay on the kitchen table. The hard cover was more wrinkled than she remembered, corners more frayed, its spiral spine a crooked snake now. Clear tabs of cellophane tape reached from the side—tiny tombstones—with names she knew well. Alice Starke. Deidre Creighton. Names that broke her heart. She flipped past pages he'd already shared with her, to new writing. Whole sentences now, not the fragments of notes he usually scribbled. Paragraphs. A story, not notes. Deidre Creighton as a child, happy, her whole life ahead of her. The description was poetry, the story cloying.

But how could he know?

The same type of fairy tale for Alice Starke, a girl who lived in a world of hurt and pain, a familiar place. She flipped through pages falling away from the spine, sat back, and ruffled the edges of the book.

He couldn't know. This is fantasy.

Her fingers touched a third tab labeled OCEAN PARK. She read.

The refrigerator clicked and quieted. The walls seemed to close in, to listen.

Conley suddenly stood next to her at the table, dressed and ready for work. She spread her fingertips on the book.

"Why did you write this?"

"I wrote these stories about Alice and Dee-Dee, and they spoke to me. They're giving me clues."

She froze. He was speaking of visions. She'd come to think of visions as the ultimate sin, the instrument that allowed one to fly too close to God. Her heart sank. His kindness, his nobility, his sacrifice, had stolen her heart these last months, and now her lover was talking about the same waking nightmares that afflicted her.

Heavy footsteps clapped up the back stairs. Muffled voices grew louder. Shawn and Hawk appeared on the landing, their faces flat and pale behind the window.

"Gina," Conley said, "listen to me. It's about to become dangerous here. You need to leave, and I need to go to Ocean Park. I'll explain when you get back from the island."

Shawn peered through the window. Hawk stood behind him like a sphinx.

"A long time ago you asked me to trust you," Conley said to her. "Now it's your turn."

Visions—people thought of them as a gift, but they were the greatest curse of all. She stared at Conley, and the concern, the earnestness in his face made her love grow even more.

Pounding at the door now, Shawn was getting angry. "C'mon Jack."

"Gina, listen to my plan," Conley repeated. "It's the only way."

He touched her face and she wished the touch would never stop. The ferry whistle blew. His hands warmed her cheeks like a blush and his eyes did not look away as he kissed her goodbye.

Chapter Thirty-Three

Conley slid onto the cold bench seat of the truck. Shawn sat in the middle, his cheek and temple whitened by the sun streaming through the windshield. Hawk climbed in the other side, and they rumbled along the dirt driveway, Hawk turning the big steering wheel with one hand.

"Gina okay?" Shawn asked. "She seemed upset."

"She's fine." He'd said it fast—too fast. They'd sensed something was wrong. Their silence was telling.

Yes, there was something so *very* wrong on so *many* levels. He'd been living for months with a woman he thought was someone else. Try explaining that to his workmates. And to make matters worse, when the veil lifted over the last few weeks and he saw *the real Gina*, he found he was smitten not just by her beauty, but by her passion and caring. He became attracted to *her*, and that brought a gnawing, senseless guilt, as if he'd betrayed his dead wife.

Hawk, Shawn, listen to this one.

The truck bounced over the uneven entrance of the driveway, and Conley straight-armed the gritty, coffee-stained dashboard for balance.

"Good to hear Gina's okay," Shawn said.

"Shawn, does Mullen know what we're doing?" Conley asked.

He laughed. "Are you crazy? Kid drinks too much

and he's got a temper uglier than my mother-in-law. No, Mullen has no clue."

"We're not ready," Hawk said. "We should wait, Shawn."

Shawn appeared not to have heard—until he spoke. "No choice. Mary says they're keeping the money in thousand-pound gun safes while they install a new time lock on the vault door on Monday." He rapped the ceiling with his knuckles. "It's now or never, that's just how it is.

"Plus we got Jackie with us, Hawk. I don't believe in banks, but I do believe in insurance." He slapped Conley on the knee. "He's our consultant. He knows how the cops think, what they'll be looking for. And he's got a powerful incentive to make us successful. Last thing a former detective wants is to be thrown into prison with a bunch of cop haters, right Jackie?"

Shawn laughed hard, just like he did when he blackmailed Jackie.

Help us or else, Matt Conley. Because I'm betting the Ocean Park police would be very interested in the whereabouts of one of their own who suddenly disappeared from the face of the earth.

They passed through downtown Harwell, Hawk upshifting deftly, the big truck groaning. Conley wondered what Hawk would do with his newfound fortune. Divorced and childless, he seemed disinterested in money. Maybe he was just here out of loyalty to Shawn.

As for Shawn, would wealth make him and his family happier? He'd rationalize and tell himself the money was earmarked for education for his kids and security for his family. But then he'd weaken and spend it on himself and Mary, and feel a strange hollowness called guilt every time he slid into his new Mercedes or checked the time on his Rolex. Thieves always pissed away money they earned too easily.

And what about him? He had no choice. In for a penny, in for a pound, Father McCarrick used to say. Conley had spent the winter keeping Luca safe from the police—and maybe a killer. He'd do what he had to, and then it was time to do more than just keep Luca safe. He needed to solve Alice Starke's murder. Neither blackmail nor the thought of jail would stop him.

****

At midnight, the blowtorch crackled as it ate through the flat asphalt roof. Conley held a flashlight over Shawn's shoulder, and red-hot chips whirled through the cone of light like a blizzard. Specks bounced off their safety glasses and stuck in the perspiration on their foreheads. Foul-smelling smoke burned their eyes. At the edge of the roof, Hawk had finished assembling the gantry and pulled it toward them, its wheels squealing and clacking.

A quarter moon sat over the sleepy, dark panorama of Harwell and cast a hazy reflection on the bay and the ferry. On Monday the town would be alert enough, everyone buzzing about the daring theft that must have been done by magicians.

When the circle Shawn had cut was almost complete, Hawk fit a pry bar into the cut and all three of them lifted the smoking upturned edge and worked it until the remaining wood cracked and the piece was free. Shawn pointed his flashlight down, illuminating the green rectangular tops of the safes. Mary hadn't failed, her measurements had placed them perfectly. All was right, but they were far from finished.

Hawk positioned the gantry over the hole. Conley helped Shawn work the one-ton chain fall attached to the gantry's cross beam, and they lowered Hawk into the bank, his chest crisscrossed with moving straps that looked like bandoliers. He used the pry bar to tilt the safe and slide the straps underneath. When he'd secured it, Hawk signaled and they pulled the hoist's hand chain until the green monster slowly rose and cleared the hole so Conley and Shawn could load it onto the dolly. Their months of back-breaking moving work made this seem easy.

They pushed the first heavy safe to the roof's edge, and Conley stole a look toward the empty street. Adrenaline had quickened his hands and heightened his senses.

What the fuck was he doing?

The next safe came faster, and it took less than twenty minutes to reposition the gantry and start lowering the vaults onto the truck. Moonlight played on the safes' glossy sides and polished levers, and one by one they settled gently onto Shawn's truck bed like an answered prayer.

Chapter Thirty-Four

Gina watched and listened at the Sunday International Food Festival.

"The cheese is spoiling, Father Bourque. The che-e-e-eze."

The old woman wrung her fat hands until the knuckles whitened, and riveted her blue eyes on the vendor's table next to her, on the few remaining cardboard bowls of poutine. The French fries looked firm, golden brown and nestled in steaming brown gravy. Gina suspected the real problem was the complaining woman's untouched wares—goulash simmered in a silver pot, a row of brats waited patiently on a painted dish, next to a full bowl of spaetzle. The Harwell festival was three hours old and evidently she'd had no takers. Her generous cheeks sagged.

"Dairy poison, Father," she pleaded to the priest. "Those women need to throw away curdled cheese. They'll kill people."

"Don't worry, Mrs. Schmidt, Mrs. LeBlanc's poutines sell too quickly to spoil."

Probably the wrong thing to say. Early afternoon and the other women were almost sold out. French-Canadian, most of them, and a few Irish. Harwell had devoured their goods—poutine, soda bread, crème brulée, corned beef, but Mrs. Schmidt's table had been passed over. Her revenge was to make sanitation an issue. Gina pitied her.

"Father, what will you do about them?" Mrs. Schmidt whined.

The other women stood at attention behind their tables, watching him deal with the outcast. They stood straight and still, remarkably nondescript in traditional dresses. Who knew skirts and blouses came in such a wide spectrum of grays, blacks, and browns? In contrast, Mrs. Schmidt's colorful wide dress and red vest made her look like an overgrown child.

"Here's what I'm going to do, Mrs. Schmidt." The priest fished his wallet from his cassock, squeezed a five-dollar bill, and laid it on the table. "I'm going to have a bowl of goulash and some spaetzle. And I'm too weak a man to resist a brat."

Her cheeks tightened and her lips parted in a smile. She filled a bowl to the brim and laid the largest sausage on a paper plate, along with egg noodles. He sipped a spoonful of soup and rolled his eyes in mock ecstasy.

Gina admired his manner. She'd seen him at Sunday Mass, and heard churchgoers talk about his character and goodness. Selfless men with noble purposes were God's finest warriors, Pura said—and she had a most challenging purpose for Father Bourque—if he accepted.

Matt had predicted he would. When he had laid out his ambitious plan for him and Gina to escape the invasion of police Harwell was about to face, Gina was skeptical. But trust meant having faith. Matt's faith in her was driven by his trust—and sealed with their love. She would not fail.

She tapped Bourque on the shoulder. "I found

you."

"Come again?"

"No, no, no," Mrs. Schmidt wailed from a distance, loud and long. She pressed a palm against her forehead, then wagged a finger at the French woman. Father's plan was backfiring. He'd empowered the German woman with his praise.

He licked grease from his fingers.

"Father," Helen LeBlanc called from the group of gathering women, "please come."

"I need confession," Gina said.

"Father Bourque," Helen pleaded, stretching his name.

He waved to her and held a glistening finger in the air.

"Confession is at 4:00," he told Gina.

His darting eyes shimmered in the midday sun.

"We need to talk, Father Bourque," she said.

He turned his back to Mrs. Schmidt and dropped the full bowl and plate in the trash. "There's a restaurant on Armitage, next to the bakery. Meet me in ten minutes."

The women were marching toward him, a black, gray, and brown parade. He wiped his mouth and hands with a napkin, spread it over the discarded food in the trash can, and made the sign of the cross.

"God willing."

****

A round metal table sat between them, with two white plates and a golden croissant on each. A waiter served tea to Gina and Bourque. The white cloth on the waiter's forearm barely moved when he set a small pitcher on the table and tapped it with clean, manicured fingertips.

"Milk, not cream, Father."

"Excellent. Thank you, Gus."

Bourque tore a small piece from his roll and turned to her.

"Pardon me, I forgot your name."

"Gina Starbird."

"Starbird. Pretty name."

He reached for the sugar bowl just as she did, and his fingers grazed the back of her hand. The touch felt strange. His fingers tingled, as if they'd touched a live wire. He pulled back.

"Sorry."

She spooned sugar into her tea and placed the bowl in front of him.

"Father, I sinned. I need penance."

"Welcome to the club, but this isn't the place for confession."

"Can you just give me penance?"

He licked his thumb, pressed it onto a flake on the dish, and held it to his lips.

"Try the croissant."

A busboy at the next table clanked dirty dishes into a plastic bin. Father sucked the crumbs off his thumb.

"God gave me a gift," she said.

"What gift?"

"I see the future. Saw the future. God took that gift away and I don't know how I offended Him."

He laughed and snapped his fingers.

"Ah, Gina, you're a fortune teller. Of course. A Gypsy."

"I never asked for the sight, Father. To me it's a curse."

He burst out laughing. The waiter stood in the doorway and studied him, brow furrowed. "Will you tell my future, Gina? Helps pay the bills, I bet. Carnivals, circus. Right? Do I get a discount? Professional courtesy and all that?"

"Please don't try to be like the others because you're not. You're different, Father Bourque."

He sipped tea.

"You're right, I'm sorry. It's been a long day."

She closed her eyes and steeled herself. "You've been chosen to help me."

"Really?" He added more sugar and stirred.

She took a long breath and grasped the side of the table. "God gave me another gift. My grandfather calls it my grace."

His eyes glistened and he smiled.

"You were here a year ago," she said. "With your mother. At this table."

"Ah, so your rearview mirror still works. Good guess, Gina. Hardly impressive. You can do better than that."

"You ordered butter croissants, just like today. For her too."

"Which is what we always ordered. No need for parlor tricks, tell me what you need from me, Gina Starbird."

She winced and covered his hands with hers. "Gabrielle died the next day."

He began to pull his hands away, then decided not to. He searched the patio and whispered, "Gus told you her name."

She squeezed. "Your mother scolded you that day, told you to order something different for a change."

Gus was at a far table, inspecting silverware and dressing down the busboy.

"Now you think "something different" was a signal," she said. "She was preparing to leave."

His hands went limp. "God in heaven," he said.

"Help me. Please, Father, help me and my brother."

He lowered his head and a tear fell onto the dish.

"You miss your mother. I didn't mean to make you cry."

He chuckled and brushed his cheeks with the backs of his hands.

"Suddenly you're not such a good mind reader, Miss Starbird. I'm not crying about my mother at all." He pushed the plate away and folded his arms. "I'm happy because I believe God is about to bless me with a task."

Chapter Thirty-Five

On Tuesday evening, Officer Claire LeJeune said, "Enter" and the door swung open. Officer McGinty limped in, trousers shivering every time he dragged his bad leg and stamped his foot. The prisoner behind him shuffled in with a different dance step. His handicap was leg irons, scraping over floor tiles and clanging like a tambourine.

Familiar young punk, another soldier in the reprobate army growing in Harwell. Street corner thugs—intimidating pedestrians, disrupting traffic. Petty criminals, mostly. Miscreants, all. A choir of liars.

This one?—he had a swagger, a carriage, a *machismo* even his clanking prison bling and orange jumpsuit couldn't emasculate.

The odd couple stared at her expectantly. She pointed to the chair on the other side of the table, the prisoner sat, and his charms rang a final ching. Not so young—wrinkles fanned from the corners of his mouth and the bountiful chest hair that curled from his V-neck collar was speckled gray.

"Prisoner's name is Mullen, Claire."

"I'll call him Prisoner, same as all the others. We won't be long, Mac."

McGinty closed the door behind him. She lifted the arrest report from the table and read.

"Good evening, Claire."

"Not in my opinion. And the name's Officer Lejeune."

He leaned forward. "I got a story to tell."

"Stories are for children, Prisoner. I prefer facts." She threw the report on the desk and tapped it with a finger. "Like the testimony of a frightened, drugged girl who awoke in your bed. Like the inventory of jewelry taken from hard-working, heartbroken people."

He shrugged. "We'll be talkin' facts, Officer Claire."

He looked toward the window and his head started to swing, to oscillate like a metronome. It suddenly stopped. "Ever wonder about jail?"

Mac's muffled voice carried from the adjoining office, a happy song. It rose, fell, and finally halted. Probably talking to his wife, Ellen, letting her know he was coming home soon.

"I never wondered," she said.

"There's two parts to it, you know."

She leaned back and checked her watch. The chair swivel creaked.

"First, there's the environment. A troubling concern when you're a newcomer—fresh fish. I'll be honest with you, one worries about that first cell, that first night. Cons call it the bridal suite for obvious reasons. Cell*mate*—think about the word, Officer Claire. Someone in the penal system had a sense of humor when they coined the term, don't you think?"

"I think only of victims, Prisoner. I'm not changing your cell. Kidnap, assault, attempted rape, grand theft? You'll be a guest of the state for quite some time with the bunkmate you drew."

"No, no, no. Don't get me wrong, Officer. That's

not what I'm asking. I'm not fresh fish. I been here more than once." His smile dimpled his cheeks.

McGinty was whistling in his office now. She might be happy too, if she had someone to go home to.

"Are we done?" she said.

"Almost." He leaned forward. "Then there's prisoner number two. He doesn't mind the cell. Teaches his roomie how the cow eats the cabbage right quick. No, number two doesn't mind what he's got. He simply hates his loss. Green grass, tree blossoms, the scent of honeysuckle. The sight of nothing but concrete can make a person crazy. I want a cell with a window, that's all I'm asking."

McGinty opened the door and stood in the threshold.

He hitched his belt and his nightstick club tapped the bad leg. "Everything all right, Missy?"

"Sure. Almost done, Mac. Start closing shop."

"How much more you gonna suffer, Claire?"

"Not much. Check back."

He left. She rose, walked to the window, and strained her wrist opening the heavy sash. She leaned on the sill anyway and ate the pain.

"Beautiful day," she said. "It'll be a balmy night, I think."

"Does it make you feel lonely? A woman in a profession of men? Do they condescend? Must be hard, always having to prove your worth."

"Mac!" she called and returned to her chair.

He leaned forward. "Okay, listen." His breath was sweet and earthy, like cloves or mint. "Casco Bank," he whispered.

"What about it?"

He folded his hands and lifted them in triumph—or prayer. The chains rattled.

"I've got a briefcase full of tips, Mullen. Every creep in this joint has a different lie. Yours won't get you sniffin' springtime."

"How'd they lift a thousand pound safe? Think, Claire, think. Who could do it?"

"Officer Lejeune."

"But I'm going to make you a star."

She called louder. "Mac, let's go. We're done."

"There's no trace because one of them is smart. Care to know his name?"

She pressed the intercom on the table, punched it three times, held it down until her finger numbed.

"Know what makes them so smart? They're insiders."

Mac came in and stood beside him. "Let's go." He slid his nightstick out of its holster, fit his hand through the strap, and rapped the back of the chair. The prisoner stood. Mac prodded him in the small of the back.

"I got names, Claire. First, last, and middle."

The guard drew back his club, knee level. "I said move it."

"Wait." Claire lowered her head and touched fingertips to temples. Mullen sat again, a thud and a chink. She looked him in the eye, assessing whether he was telling the truth. She glanced at McGinty, poised, face turned toward her, questioning. She placed the arrest report on the corner of the table.

"Bring me paper and pencil, McGinty." She sat straight, pushed the intercom away, planted elbows on the table, and folded her hands. "And you better call Ellen again. We'll be working late."

Chapter Thirty-Six

Machines were such sorry markers. People cherished cars, computers, gadgets and gizmos so dearly they never forgot them. Sad state of affairs when the touch of cold metal and plastic triggered nostalgia.

Later that night, Claire lifted the scanner's cover and placed the license photo of the man Mullen had named—Jack Smith.

Here's a memory in the making.

The scanner hummed quietly.

People. Friends. Lovers—they should be making memories, not machines. Damn contraptions were becoming ubiquitous, but soulmates?—not so much. Unfair. Machines could beguile with noise and lights, but an old friend—okay, one who might have become more than a friend—only beckoned in dreams.

Probably for the best.

She saved the image to her laptop, attached it to an email, and studied the picture of Jack Smith on her screen.

Was Mullen telling the truth about this stranger—and was Smith even his real name? Or was this a gambit, a wasted effort? Nothing ventured, nothing gained. She'd see if he had a rap sheet elsewhere in the Northeast first. Just playing the odds. Mullen said Jack Smith was arrogant, and people of that persuasion usually hailed from New England or New York.

Southerners claimed the Civil War—*The War of Northern Aggression*—brought an end to manners in America, and an honest Northerner wouldn't disagree.

She searched her address list for Hartford P.D. Albany next, then Boston. She wondered who was opening their email. Probably some other neurotic soul with nothing better to do on a Sunday night.

Click. Click. Click.

Better get used to the sound, it might be the future—no more physical contact, just people passing their pictures around the globe, with captions, and never having to speak their true feelings.

Claire from Maine here, passionate servant of the people of Harwell. Cat lover. Gemini. Constant companion of a remarkable priest she thinks about way too much.

****

Massachusetts state troopers stormed Jack Smith's apartment the next morning. They looked like giants, muscles straining against blue shirts and leather crossbelts, their jackboots clattering like horse hooves. They toppled a dresser and it landed with a thunderclap. They crouched, opened drawers, and searched inside and under the emptied frame.

"Tell your men to stand down," Claire yelled in Captain Roland Gerard's face.

It had taken only a day to get a response to her query—a very swift and forceful response.

"Watch your shoulder," he answered as one trooper edged past with a drawer full of clothes. The vein in the man's neck bulged and his black hair gleamed with sweat.

The blue monsters' caps hung on pegs beside the

back door. She wished they'd fetch them and leave. One was turning the drawer over the kitchen table now, and clothes tumbled out, unfolding in mid-air and bunching in a pile. The other mutant was still tossing the bedroom, wrestling with the mattress. The box spring went next, slamming the floor like a hammer.

"You're not in the Bay State, Captain." She lowered her voice until it was measured and controlled. "You're in the great state of Maine."

"A beautiful commonwealth."

"Of which you are a guest."

"And an appreciative one."

"You asked to see his apartment, Captain, not tear it apart."

His jaw twitched. "Time's against us, Ms. Lejeune."

One of his men came out of the bedroom, scribbling on a clipboard.

"I'll want a copy of the inventory," she said.

A car's horn blared in the distance. Birds chattered in the nearby trees.

"Has he no voice, Captain? Is he mute? Tell him to answer me."

"He answers to me." He held up the picture she'd sent him. "Where's this Jack Smith now?"

"He works at a bar named Cronin's near the waterfront."

Clothes from the closet next, shoes and shirts. The nightstand drawer was emptied of books, toiletries, keys. Junk drawers from the kitchen were overturned on the table. Gerard sifted through the pile, inspecting bills, ads, and receipts. He picked up a ticket, playing-card sized, and read. He found more of the same and held them to her, fanned like a poker hand.

"What are these?"

She hesitated, picked one, and held it to the light.

"Tickets for the ferry—to Baker Island."

Everyone froze. Three statues gazed at her, their sudden stillness unsettling. He cleared space on the table and pulled out a chair. He tore a clean page from his man's clipboard and clicked a pen ready. She sat. He opened her hands with his calloused ones and wrapped her fingers around the pen.

"I need to know about this island and this ferry."

Why had she sat so quickly? Why did her hand tremble? Why was her voice so small?

He turned to his men. "I'll meet you in the morning at the ferry. I have unfinished business first."

Claire composed herself. "The fruit of this search is inadmissible in court."

"Doesn't matter," Gerard said. "We're officers of the law, Officer Lejeune." He leaned forward and warm breath touched her cheek. The brim of his cap cast a diagonal shadow across his face and darkened one eye. He whispered, "We're the true agents of justice."

****

Plymouth Gin, the good stuff. VO. Canadian Club. Fleischmann's?—that soldier didn't belong on the top shelf. That night, Conley lifted the bottles by their sticky necks and inventoried them on a clipboard. He arranged the bottles in the speed rack and they clinked like a toast.

"You're working too hard."

Oakie again, slumped on a stool, elbows on the bar. Legs hung limply over the seat, toes of his soiled sneakers pointing at the floor. Black and yellow teeth grinned proudly.

"I told you the bar is closed." Conley opened the beer chest and counted the remaining bottles.

"Door's open. I'm sentimental today, Jackie. I can't believe old man Cronin's dead. He said he wanted me to toast him when he kicked. Grab a couple of those depth charges in the chest, will you? One for both of us."

"Not gonna happen. Cronin's kids are in charge now. Bar's closed for the night."

Oakie dragged the back of his hand across his lips. "Just one drink. Quit bein' such a boy scout. Living on the street is thirsty work, you know."

Conley reached for a mug, poured tap water, and slid the glass to him. "Best I can do."

Oakie lifted the mug. "Well, then. Here's to the old man. You done good, Cronie. Forty years of serving the town of Harwell."

"Forty years of calcifying livers."

"Don't be like that." Oakie laughed, drained the glass, and dragged his arm under his bulbous nose. He reached over the bar and pressed the draught beer tap. Beer poured onto a silver grill and foamed. "Okay, forget the cooler, Jack. How about a pull from the keg? Clean the lines out. We'll be doin' ole Cronin a favor."

"No way."

"You saying we can't salute the old man?"

He looked at the open doorway. Dust motes swirled in the light of the streetlamp. He grabbed Oakie's mug and poured beer from the tap.

"You do that real good," he purred and licked his lips. "Some guys got the touch, most don't."

"Last drink, this is it."

"Absolutely." He lifted the glass. "Cronie was a gentleman, worked hard his whole life. Most will remember him for lukewarm beer and watered-down whiskey, but he was solid. Lucky bugger went to bed one night and woke up dead. Best way to go."

A car droned by. The beer tap dripped.

"That was a nice eulogy," Conley said, one eye on the door. Where the hell were Shawn and Hawk? "You earned another." He refilled the mug.

"He reminded me of you, Jack. High integrity, no time for foolishness." He downed half and suddenly leaned forward. The spiderweb veins in his cheeks bulged. Stomach growled a disturbing slosh. He rubbed his belly, belched, smiled, and spoke.

"Last couple of the day always go down hard."

Conley went outside and scanned the long, empty boulevard of asphalt that stretched to the horizon on the left. On the right, it disappeared under a railroad bridge. Bums slept underneath, away from streetlights, covered with dirty blankets and cardboard, surrounded by trash bags and bottles.

He checked his watch. Shawn was late. Hawk had finally cracked open the safe and divided the money, and as soon as Conley received his share, he'd leave for Ocean Park. He went back inside.

Oakie's mug was fuller and darker—a fifth of Old Thompson's sat next to it. He stared at his drink lovingly, lifted it high, and finished the boilermaker. He climbed down from the stool and stumbled to the door and out.

Back to work. Conley set a case of beer next to the cooler and transferred bottles into the cold, greasy water. Icy water ran down his arm and wet his sleeve.

When a shadow fell over him, he stood. A new visitor occupied Oakie's stool, one with bright eyes, a white smile, and spearmint breath.

"Roland Gerard. What took you so long?"

"I knew you weren't dead, Conley."

The old cop tipped his hat back and glassware reflected on his high forehead. His skin was taut and unwrinkled, uniform crisp and creased, as always. A ruby ring glistened on his pinky, and his Seawatch chronograph gleamed.

"How does it feel to be born again, Jack Smith? Not many are blessed with a second chance. I visited your new home this morning. Do you appreciate your gift, your new life? Every life ends. Is it comforting to know when?" He removed the watch, pressed the button at the two o'clock position, and laid it on the bar. The second hand swept steadily and the orange minute hand tracked slower. Three subdials looked like round eyes and an open mouth on a face.

"Where's Angelo?" Conley said.

"Partnerships—they all end the same. Starts with joint interest and ends with a lesson in self-reliance. Angelo lost interest. He's Chief of Detectives now. Sends his regards to you and your fortune-telling whore."

"He lost interest? Impossible."

"Believe it."

Conley slid the beer chest lid closed. "No."

"Is the Gypsy on Baker Island?" Gerard asked.

"Forget about it, he's innocent."

Gerard smiled. "Makes me want him even more."

Conley picked up his jacket, fished his truck keys from the pocket, came around the bar, and stood next to

Gerard.

"You never disappoint, Captain, but you're wasting time here. Have a nice trip back."

Gerard's hand suddenly dropped to his belt. Metal flashed and he clamped the open cuff of a come-along on Conley's wrist. When he spoke, his eyes were electric.

"You're wanted for questioning, Detective Matt Conley, for aiding and abetting Gypsy scum. I should take you in. But your cozy new life doesn't have to end yet. Is Starbird on the island?"

"Send Angelo. I'll tell him."

Gerard unloosed the billy club from his belt, swung it in an arc, and smashed Conley's shoulder. He yanked at the cuffs to get away, and blood trickled from the cuts it made on his wrists.

A truck engine growled in the distance. Conley turned sideways, eyes on the stick, and the manacle tore his flesh even more. Gerard had more to say.

"Loyalty's overrated," Gerard hissed. "Here's some advice, Conley. Surrender and beg forgiveness. That sometimes works."

Brakes squealed—twice. Outside, the truck engine roared. He looked to the street. A behemoth had finally arrived—not Shawn, but a rumbling dump truck that darkened the doorway for an instant, upshifted, and sped past.

Another swing of the club. He ducked and felt its wind. Suddenly a voice called to them from the doorway.

"You closed or not, Jackie? I see a customer."

Oakie stood in the doorway, a silhouette in the glow of streetlights behind him. His face was ashen and spittle shone on his chin. He clapped a tire iron into his palm and stepped forward. Another black cutout entered behind him, holding a car antenna against his leg. More bums from the bridge filtered in slowly, armed with jagged, broken bottles. They fanned around the bar.

"Don't forget," Oakie said, "I get the last drink."

The bar was quiet with the eerie, still silence that anticipates the next word—or action. Gerard swore, then slowly removed the come-along and returned it to his belt. His eyes had lost their iridescence. Blood streamed across Conley's hand.

The ragtag army drifted toward the bar, shuffling in loose, battered shoes. Their faces were worn and tan, dirt caked in pores and creases, and eyes glowed as yellow as butter. Long hair and beards were tangled corkscrews. The aroma of stale booze and body odor grew with their advance.

Shawn's truck pulled up outside. He honked for Conley.

Oakie waved Conley away.

"You take off, Jackie. Me and the Captain here will have one more toast. To old man Cronin."

Chapter Thirty-Seven

A bad sign, that moving compass. The next morning, Gerard watched it spin and wobble, its hash marks blending into a white blur. Just trying to do its job, unaware it had no job when the ferry was docked, its lines tied to the jetty. High wind was the culprit, rocking the ship, tricking the instruments.

Wasted tonnage.

Hard to argue. The *Casco Lady's* destination—Baker Island—lay in plain sight, a mass wide enough to fill the horizon, close enough to distinguish hovering sea gulls from terns. Yes, depth gauges and magnetic navigation gadgets were not needed for this bee-line trip.

The ferry suddenly swayed, its dock lines creaked, and the black compass ball spun fast, like a giant marble in oil. The ship's wheel began to twitch, and Gerard's troopers, riding in the wheelhouse so as not to frighten passengers with their arsenal of guns, shifted impatiently from one foot to the other. Their rifle barrels, pointed at the deck, drew lazy circles.

"Trouble on the island?" the ferry captain, a man named Dumars, asked him.

Gerard raised his chin and fixed him with stern eyes. Last night's episode with Conley at the bar still gnawed at him. "Just get us there."

Dumars nodded, cleared his throat, and leaned to

the voice tube. "Secure the vessel." His voice competed with distant thunder. "Cast off."

A sheet of rain pelted the wheelhouse roof and sluiced down its windows to the kent screens. The downpour dimpled the water in front of the bow and, just as suddenly, the squall disappeared. Dumars pushed the power lever forward, the boat lurched, and the rifle barrels drew larger circles. A shotgun, its muzzles dark as ink and big as silver dollars, barely moved. A blast of the horn was followed by an exhaust cloud floating past the wheelhouse. The ferry launched and they departed Harwell for its baby island. Away from the berth, into Casco Bay, into a swirl of currents that twisted and spun like a blue kaleidoscope. Milky whitecaps, as immaculate as the boil under the cutwater, dotted the harbor. The ship slid sideways, the undertow pulling it toward the north part of the bay.

Gerard stepped forward and spread a nautical chart over the helm. Dumars' eyes widened before he spoke.

"I ain't seen a chart like this since maritime school—circled buoy markers, double and triple-digit sounding numbers." His fingertips touched places on the chart before he used them to rub his chin. "I don't use them as a rule, and this one looks suspect anyway. Nun buoy on latitude 85? Not anymore. That particular bobber was blown away by a nor'easter years ago. Fifty-foot sounding in the south bay? It's at least 100. I gauge depths and currents by feel, Officer, by instinct, by sound, by the tune the props sing in the chop."

Gerard pointed at a place on the map and the sway of the boat made his hand waver.

"This island," he said. "Where are its egresses?"

"Its what?"

Gerard shook his head. His men grinned.

"Exits. How many ways can one leave the island?

Dumars tapped the round, lollipop cove with the narrow entrance. "Only here." He drew his finger along a fold to the landing dock, just above the compass rose. "Baker's just a rock, really, used to be called Egg Rock. Windward is unnavigable."

"Windward?"

Dumars leaned toward Gerard's right ear and spoke—slowly, clearly, loud enough for his men to hear.

"Ocean side. Exposed to the Atlantic. Basic seamanship, Captain Gerard. Even an ebb tide will drive a craft against the cliffs. Take a special sailor to beat it."

Another fart of diesel smoke drifted by and fouled the wheelhouse.

"And here?" Gerard touched the narrow end of the island and the paper crinkled.

"Worse. The bay fights the tide and spins a boat like a top. Creates vortices, whirlpools. If you could avoid them, if you could land, then you deal with cliffs. In bad weather, it's suicide. And the south?—sea rocks will punch a hole in the strongest hull."

Baker Island loomed ahead. Waves pounded the cliffs, loud as cannon fire. The island grew and the cove entrance widened. A handful of boats rocked inside. Rain clouds darkened the currents to playful, shifting shades of gray. Dumars idled the diesel and they coasted. A touch of reverse, a pull on the wheel. The ferry slid sideways, slapped the island jetty, and the *Casco Lady* let out a quiet groan.

****

The ramp slammed onto the dock and Gerard's men followed him off, footsteps ringing the metal walk like a church bell. Passengers filed by, pretending not to stare. Good to be on land, even this treeless, desolate spit full of seagulls and the stench of dead fish. Why had Starbird chosen this God-forsaken refuge?

The question likely contained its answer.

A man approached, a forlorn soul in a loose khaki uniform and scuffed black sneakers with broken backs. Vacant eyes searched from a soft face. His brass nametag read Benson.

"Benson?" Gerard said. "Where are your men?"

"Men? Me and Riley's the only code enforcement officers, Captain Gerard, that's all there is. He's up watching the killa like you ordered."

"Where is up?"

Benson pointed to a half dozen homes with gingerbread trim and flowers in window boxes. A cliff was their backyard, dotted with moss, draped with vines.

"Just over that ridge. Your man Luke's holed up in an old fishing shack on the nasty side of the rock."

"Luca," Gerard corrected.

"We've got eyes on him, Riley does anyway."

"What's his plan?"

Brow furrowed, Benson shrugged, and his squat neck disappeared into his rounded shoulders.

"Riley? He ain't got no plan. He's watchin' the killa, just like you told him to."

Gerard studied the cliff. "Did the Gypsies see him?"

"No," Benson confided, stretching the word, the twitch of a smile on the corners of his mouth. "No way.

Riley's real good."

"Stay here," Gerard said to his closest man.

"No need," Benson said. "Killa's in the fishin' shack, me and Riley both seen him." He surveyed the armed men and patted his holstered gun. "We need all the guns you got. We only got pistols."

Gerard studied the shine on his boots and looked up at the expectant stare of a half dozen sets of eyes. He smiled at his host. "You win, Officer. Show us the way."

Benson turned and his bowlegs motored with an odd, mechanical gait, step and swing. They followed past a general store and a post office, door hardware corroded with rust, shingles salt-stained and bleached gray.

They marched along a narrow asphalt road, single-file, on a bike path bordered by a white traffic line. Ragweed, gently swaying, bent toward them. Surf battered the breakwall on the other side of the road. They cradled their rifles at port arms, muzzles aimed at light blue sky over deep blue ocean. A breeze blew constant, thick with the musty smell of salt.

A boy rode by on a bike, craned backward to gape, and pedaled hard.

Benson wiped his brow and slowed. His shirt back was soaked from perspiration. Struggling from a simple walk? They were about the same age, Gerard and Benson, same height, similar build. Same features even, but there the similarity ended.

Iron sharpens iron, and when there's none available to do the chore, the spirit and body dull. Benson was a good bad example, an object lesson, a warning, a carbon copy of Gerard minus experience, education, and intelligence.

Off the road, into a break in the weeds, and they climbed a great sloping rock painted with guano and pocked with puddles. Benson teetered at the steep parts before they finally crested the rock. Gerard never teetered. That was one benefit of a fanatical exercise routine, disciplined habits, and self sacrifice. A body that fought back the deterioration of age because he didn't allow it. At sixty, he was more fit than Benson at thirty.

A shack lay ahead, almost lost in the ominous rain clouds collecting behind it. Benson led them to a crop of high boulders and they gathered behind a man who stood watch. Tall and thin, he wore the same uniform as Benson, but with creases.

"Riley, where's the perp?" Benson said.

"Around the side. He's been in and out of the shack."

"Are you sure it's Starbird?" Gerard asked.

Riley reached into his back pocket and brought out a square of paper. He unfolded the packet and stretched it, top and bottom, with wizened, grubby fingers—the mug shot of Luca Starbird. "Borrowed this picture from the post office bulletin board. I recognized him right off, and I can count the stitches on a fastball. He jerked his head toward the shack. "Starbird's in there, Captain Gerard. That's your man."

Another castaway, this Riley. Check that—not a castaway, more likely the progeny of backward Maine islanders, just like his partner. Mentally deficient because they were never mentally challenged. Exile a man—*men*—to an island and one might as well strike them from the human race.

Riley's eyes suddenly widened and a reflection changed his pupils from black to red. He looked toward the shack and shouted a word.

"Fire!"

Flame shot from the side of the shack and over the roof, great licks tipped with jets of black smoke. They turned and ran in unison, clattering over turd-stained rocks, splashing through black puddles.

Add arsonist to the many faces of Luca Starbird. Murderer, thief, kidnapper?—meet firebug.

They passed the shack to a bonfire burning on the other side, a mound of furniture, kitchenware, framed pictures, clothes, and roiling smoke that tasted like hickory. A pyramid of wood supported the mess, crisscrossed two-by-fours that flames licked in and around. Gerard ran back to the shack and kicked the front door once, twice, crack, and open. His men's rifles pointed at the doorway.

The old Gypsy lay still in a narrow bed, dressed in a white suit and purple tie, eyes closed, arms crossed. A small table next to his head held a battered hat and three stacks of coins. Flowers draped his bedposts, fat, colorful blossoms on strings like Hawaiian leis.

They filed into the shack, across the empty, scarred wooden floor to bare cupboards and empty closets. The fire outside was a pyre of everything that should be inside. Sheets hung from the wall. Gerard tore one away and confronted his startled face in a mirror.

The old man was dead.

"There!" Benson shouted outside. "There!"

Gerard joined him.

"That's him," Riley shouted. "That's Starbird."

At the bottom of the cliff, a man in oilskins sat in a

red dory, pushing against the cliff with an oar. He caught an ebb, turned his boat, and paddled to sea.

"Put out the fire," Gerard told his men. "Stay here, he might double back. He's a schemer."

Benson peered down the slope. A wave exploded against the cliff. "This scheme will kill him."

"He can't die," Gerard said. "Not yet."

Benson lifted his head. The wind was strong enough to lean into. "Ay-uh. Then we better go get him."

****

They went back to the coast road, double time. Gerard led, Riley following close, Benson in the rear. Down the plateau, through the ragweed, onto the street. A truck blasted its horn and gave a wide berth. They trekked downhill, back to the cove, to a 25-foot twin-engine Boston Whaler docked in the shadow of the ferry. *BAKER* was stenciled on the hull in green block letters. The boat had a high bow and a wide beam, its brightwork shiny and dry under the center console's canopy. Benson leaped from the dock to the deck of the rocking boat, no hands. He keyed the ignition, cranked the controls, and the outboards' props bubbled to smoky life. Riley freed a dock line from one cleat, his skinny arms and legs working like a spider's, and he scurried to the next. He shouted over the engine noise.

"We'll have to haul him on board. He won't last long out there."

The engines roared, the bow of the Whaler rose, its stern dropped, and they shot forward. Lightning flashed, thunder cracked, and rain came, thrashing, driving, and cold. Gerard held the slippery gunwales with both hands.

The rain formed a silver curtain around a foreboding cove ahead, a black corner of cliffs. Jagged rocks rose, washed by crashing waves. Benson palmed the power lever and held it, hand vibrating, knuckles white. The twin props dug a deeper trough. Benson's trousers flapped, but his bowlegs stood firm, spread like a wishbone, his feet anchored to the deck. His turtle head pivoted, searching the horizon.

From the hill above, Gerard's men watched the rescue. The bonfire flames were gone, replaced by a column of white smoke billowing like steam from a cauldron. Waves pounded the boat. He concentrated, trying to time them and brace himself as the swells rolled like heaving blue blankets. His gorge shifted, a nauseating slosh, and he belched. Spray covered him and his clothes became a second set of skin, seal-slick and cold. Drenched from above and below, he wondered if he'd drown inside the boat.

Benson ran the gauntlet deftly, fast tacks, turning and splitting every wave that threatened to hit broadside. Forward, idle, reverse. They seemed to be moving on a giant hand, spinning like a tilt-a-whirl.

In the distance, Starbird's boat rode a cresting wave. Oars reached toward the water, but the paddles fanned only air. The bow plunged into a hole and rose again, covered with white froth. An oar slipped out of its lock and disappeared. The rocks shone, prisms of color playing off the black pillars.

Closer. It seemed impossible Benson could even approach the tossing rowboat.

Closer. Starbird swung his single oar.

The Whaler spun, the dory rose, and the oilskin rowman suddenly stood, hands open to them. Starbird had lost weight since the last time Gerard had seen him. His frame was slighter, hair graying, and he'd grown a thin mustache.

Riley threw an orange life preserver on a rope, and it floated over Starbird's head and splashed behind. The dory rocketed away toward twin rocks.

Riley was pulling the rope back when Benson shouted and handed him binoculars. He used them.

"It's not Starbird," he yelled.

Gerard's head was starting to spin, and his hands trembled. He sat on the deck and cold sea water soaked his pants and paralyzed his legs. The inbreds were talking nonsense, nonsense that needed to stop. If only he could stand, or at least rise to all fours.

"No," he croaked. "That's impossible. It's Starbird."

"It's not Starbird. Christ Almighty, Christ Almighty," Riley hollered and blessed himself, dripping-wet fingers touching dripping-wet forehead, chest, shoulders. "It's the priest from the mainland. It's Father Bourque."

More of the miscreants' rantings.

So tired.

"Throw it again," Benson yelled, working the Whaler like a bucking horse. "Make this one good, Riley." He maneuvered perilously close to the twin peaks and reversed. The boat wrenched.

Gerard felt nauseous as the boat stopped, started, stopped, started.

The lasso arced behind the ring—a spinning orange bird that seemed to hang in the air until providence laid its trailing rope over the dory. The rowman stood again, palms to the sky as if catching the rain.

Cold sweat trickled between Gerard's shoulder blades.

Hard to breathe. So tired.

"Grab the ring," one of the dullards shouted. "Grab the ring, Father."

He needed correcting. "Starbird," Gerard said. He struggled to his knees and hung over the side, faced a pale reflection of himself in blue water, and hurled.

****

Soon after, the ferry's gangplank ratcheted onboard and dropped to the deck with a clang. Gina's tears would not stop. The brim of Luca's hat shaded his eyes. She led him to the bench behind the wheelhouse and he placed his arm around her.

"Who do you cry for?" he said.

She smiled. Grandfather's words, Grandfather's game.

I already miss you, Pura. I cry for you.

Why? I'm in a better place.

I cry for the past—you, me, and little Luca.

We all have to grow up. Who do you cry for, Gina?

She wiped her eyes.

I cry for me.

The pier receded behind them, brown suds slapping the pilings and washing onto gray boards. A muffled command came from the wheelhouse and the ferry began to move. Baker Island grew small, framed by the ship's flat wake. White smoke rose from the other side of the island. The rain was ending, dark clouds thinning, the sky lightening. They traveled faster. Halfway to the mainland, the wind blew and the ferry shuddered. She clutched her brother's arm with both hands and held on tight.

Chapter Thirty-Eight

"What the hell was Remi doing in a rowboat, Claire? He couldn't swim."

"I don't know, Roger."

Claire and Father Bourque's brother Roger stalked the waiting room at the Harwell General Emergency Ward. Roger seemed to be over her shoulder every time she turned.

"You must have some idea," Roger said. "You were his friend."

She raised a hand. "Friend, not keeper."

She'd never felt so happy in her life. Father Remi Bourque had been miraculously saved from the harbor in a howling storm. Professionalism was the only thing stopping her from crying tears of joy and maybe even kissing the two island safety officers who'd rescued him. His prognosis was good and he'd even squeezed her hand and smiled at her in the ambulance, the most wonderful feeling she'd ever had. A miracle.

Roger hung at her shoulder, still throwing questions. He looked like his brother—sharp nose, florid cheeks, intense, tracking eyes. More of his kin were in the lobby, a gauntlet she wanted to avoid. Her phone dinged, and she read a text and hurried out the side exit.

Phil Lyman stood in front of his cruiser, badge gleaming, shoes and gun belt polished, shirttail hanging over his butt.

"He's packing up, getting ready to leave."

"Who?"

"Conley."

Conley. The name had become a shouted cuss, a crashing cymbal, an insult to the ear. He may not have been the cause of Remi's near miss and all the heartache visited on Harwell, but his name was a constant in the conversation.

"Just follow him, Phil."

Lyman wrung his hands until the knuckles whitened. He looked like he was ready to pray.

"What if he crosses the county line? Or the state?"

"Jesus, Phil, make a decision for once in your life."

"What decision, Claire?"

She touched fingertips to her forehead, then folded her arms.

"Give me the keys to the cruiser. I'm driving."

"What about Father Bourque?"

She looked back at the Emergency entrance. She so wanted to talk to Father again, to touch his face. Reluctantly, she turned to Phil and opened her hand.

"Keys."

****

Claire and Phil Lyman parked under an oak tree near Conley's apartment and waited, unseen. A breeze rustled the branches and an acorn struck the roof of the car with a startling bang.

"Should we just arrest Conley? There's a warrant."

"No, Phil. He might be going to the money."

"Look. There he is."

A man in a ball cap shut his back door and trotted down the stairs, dufflebag slung over the shoulder. He threw the bag in the truck cab, started the engine, and smoke rose from a noisy exhaust pipe. He lowered the driver's window and rested his arm on the door.

She shifted into gear and followed at a distance. They wound through the narrow streets, past tenements and gin mills, the seedy part of Harwell. He did the speed limit and stopped at every sign. Passed the factory on the outskirts of Harwell, to the highway. She kept her distance, the pulsing hum of their engines rising and falling. He suddenly passed a car and sped ahead. She accelerated.

What the hell was Remi doing in a rowboat?

I bet Conley knows, Roger. Ask Matt Conley.

"We're gonna lose him," Phil said.

"Shut up."

"What did you say?"

"You heard me."

"Claire, just radio ahead for help. You'll kill us."

He slipped the cruiser's microphone out of its holder. She reached to the console and shut the radio.

Onto the interstate.

The off ramp near the new mall was spitting cars onto the highway, and they quickly blocked all three lanes. She cut to the passing lane. Conley's truck was two cars up, barely visible, just a black fender. Suddenly a suitcase bounced out of the truck, cartwheeled on the highway, and burst open, empty. Its shiny green lining flashed a final farewell before one car crushed the case under its tires, then another.

She pulled within inches of the bumper in front of her. Phil put his hand on the wheel. "Easy," he shouted.

She slapped him away and pulled to the side of the road, tires rumbling to a stop on the rough shoulder.

"What's wrong, Claire?"

"Get out."

She reached past him, elbow on his belly, opened the door, and pushed against his shoulder. Phil grunted and did a full rotation in the seat, tumbled out, and landed on all fours on the long green grass of a berm. He struggled to stand. She stepped on the gas and burned rubber, and the door slammed shut on its own. Back on the highway. Cars swerved away. Phil's reflection stared at her in the rearview mirror, a man two inches tall with limp arms and a pale face. She leaned on the horn and a startled driver jerked to the next lane. The jam got worse. Cars moved painfully slow, in tight formation. She tailgated a station wagon and honked again. Finally they slowed and separated, and she shot past. The truck had disappeared.

She floored the gas pedal and the cruiser's engine blatted like a hot rod. She slowed as she passed a rest area and scanned the few cars there—no black truck. An eighteen wheeler was coming out the exit and he pumped his air brakes when she cut him off.

There. There he was, tooling along in the travel lane. She pulled aside, waved him over, and parked behind. She shut the engine and popped the trunk. Took the shotgun from the rack, broke open the barrels and saw the reassuring sight of the shell rims inside. She marched to the driver, muzzle pointed at the breakdown lane marker.

She'd been beside herself when the call about Remi came in. An annoying tear kept tickling her cheek and she kept grinding it away with her palm.

Remi's alive. He could have died.

Traffic had slowed again, this time to watch her.

She raised the shotgun and pointed the fat muzzles at the driver. His eyes grew on his wide moon face, a face she'd never seen before.

No thanks to you.

"What'd I do?"

"Where's Matt Conley?"

"Who? My name's Shawn Sullivan, ma'am."

Everything was quiet now. Cars slowed, drivers gawked. Exhaust billowed, rich and greasy.

"Get out."

"Why?"

She held the gun steady, stock against her shoulder, its coldness seeping through her shirt. He stepped down, his open hands framing his frightened face.

She lowered the gun, stepped past him, and looked in the cab. She searched for the full duffle bag the man leaving Conley's apartment had cradled like a baby, close to his chest. The passenger seat held an open newspaper, the floor an empty Styrofoam cup.

The driver spoke from behind, his voice loud and clear against the drone of traffic.

"Don't believe I know any Conleys, ma'am. Name sounds familiar, though. Matt Conley, you say?"

Chapter Thirty-Nine

That night, heavy traffic sped by on the other side of the highway median, dark creatures with white luminescent eyes that grew like slow starbursts. They flared just before they passed, as if in warning. Their number seemed endless.

Conley turned Shawn's truck onto the long, winding exit ramp to Ocean Park. His headlights lit cracked concrete curbs, weeds, and grime. He straightened the wheel on the wide boulevard that led to the city he came from, and prepared himself. He was about to make good on his promise to Gina. He drove downtown, through geometrical shadows cast by streetlamps and into sleepy neighborhoods, bungalows and old colonials with tired, sagging roofs and porches. He reached the lake in Ocean Park Woods, and the great forest surrounding it, and parked.

Stone pillars stood sentry at the woods' entrance, connected by a rusty chain. He ducked under. Trash was strewn on the dirt road—yellowed newspapers, billowing plastic bags. The ruts were deeper than before, filled with black mud that clawed his shoes like quicksand. A full moon lit the big pines on both sides. The spiky, swaying boughs seemed alive.

He followed the path to the long, grassy steps he'd climbed eleven months before. Into the rose garden. Flowers were dead or dying, and brown leaves and faded petals formed a floor of mulch that stank like rotting meat. He parted the branches of the firs Angelo had touched so long ago. The brook ran quietly. He remembered finding Alice on thick, dark ferns, but now realized it was actually a bed of moss. He searched the branches overhead and touched the green shoots that had replaced the broken ends.

He crossed the brook, pretended Alice was still there, and stood above the place they'd found her. Water murmured over smooth rocks. Angelo was less than ten feet away that day, face in a notebook, asking obvious questions, his hand writing furiously. Did his eyes blink? Did he look up?

He wrote.

Did he move at all? Did he breathe?

He simply wrote.

He walked to the spot where his partner had stood, turned, and looked back at the moss bed.

Time to go. Time to see Angelo.

****

At dawn, the windows in Angelo's hilltop house glimmered, reflecting the ocean like mirrors. Conley parked at the beach and climbed the access road. The sun had cleared the horizon, a peach-colored balloon rising in a cloudless sky, and created an unseasonably warm April day. The thick, salt-laden air lay on his face like a compress. Seagulls cawed, waves crashed gently, and a breeze carried the sickly-sweet smell of lilac. He climbed wooden steps and knocked on a weathered door.

"Angelo." He slammed the door with his palm. "Angelo, it's me."

His hand tingled, and his voice sounded husky and

foreign. Sweat trickled inside his collar. He raised the hand again.

The door swung open. Angelo stood in front of him, squinting.

"Conley?"

The dark eyes flickered, then the familiar surly stare returned, along with the commanding voice.

"Wait here," he said and disappeared into a hallway.

Conley stepped inside. Dust motes danced in shafts of light filtering through Venetian blinds. The place was spartan. An old sofa was the only furniture, draped with a throw, positioned to the view. A door slammed shut. Angelo appeared again, wearing a leather jacket. He stood in the sunbeams and lit a cigarette. He looked the same. Neither time nor trouble had changed Danny Angelo's appearance, his clean-shaven face, and his creased clothes. He shuffled past without a word, down the steps, and Conley followed. They descended the winding road.

Angelo busied himself smoking. None of his chatter today, his incessant opinions, observations, commentary, and pontifications. Their shoes slapped the asphalt as they marched to the beach and stood watching the surf.

"I figured it out," Conley said. "You were scared of Gina's clairvoyance, scared she'd see your sins. That's why you didn't come to Maine with Gerard. She only needs to touch someone's hand to read their soul. Tell me about Alice Starke."

Angelo kicked off his shoes and stretched. Seconds ticked by. The long silence was his confession.

"You had to be the one to find Alice's body so you

could explain your footprints being there," Conley said. "You needed the autopsy report to make sure they found no DNA."

Angelo took the butt from his mouth and talked with his hand, and the burning tip left tiny trails of smoke.

"Don't cry for her, Conley. Alice Starke was a junkie and a pusher. She killed a kid who muled for her. Gave him a fentanyl hot shot. She would have killed others."

"Trying to convince me—or yourself?"

His head snapped sideways. The old Angelo was back, quick and testy.

"What would you do? Would you have the courage to save many lives by taking one?"

"Courage? You killed her, Angelo, and mutilated her."

Angelo spoke louder. "Easy to do nothing, Conley. Easy to let these conniving losers and sluts think they'll live forever."

He threw the end of the cigarette in the sand and walked into the water. The surf buffeted his legs, but he trudged steadily, until he was knee deep. Conley waited. The water had to be frigid and numbing. Maybe that was the point.

When Angelo finally returned, his pants clung to his legs.

"What about Deidre?" Conley said. "What did she do wrong?"

Angelo took his time answering. "Nothing, really. Except maybe hate her miserable small town life. Ever stand at the edge of a cliff and feel the urge to jump, Conley? That's what it's like. Killing. Something inside telling you to do her, to end it for her. And when her skin's like velvet and her face is angelic…whoa, the feeling's even stronger." Angelo's voice deepened. "It was that urge again, Conley. A glorious thing. Must be how addicts feel. Nothing's more important than the next rush. She was just ripe for the picking."

"But the sticks. The sticks, Angelo."

Angelo simply lit another cigarette.

"You couldn't look at their eyes," Conley ventured. "You didn't have that kind of courage."

"That's where you're wrong, Conley. That was my nobility. My humanity showing. What would you think of a man who could ignore those pleading eyes?"

Conley's stomach roiled. But he'd come here for a reason.

"Luca Starbird did nothing to either of these women, Angelo. Save him."

But Angelo only shook his head. "You never change, do you, my friend? Always got to do the right thing. But therein lies the beauty of my circumstances. They'll never catch a man like Starbird, and they'll chase him forever." He took a long drag of his cigarette, and inhaled deeply before exhaling again. "But this is about his sister, isn't it? She's *your* cross, only you haven't figured that out yet." He tossed the cigarette aside, unfinished. "You should forget her, Conley, but you can't. One of those damn urges again. If she were here, I'd kill her for you. For old time's sake." He smiled. "Instead, I'll just have to do the next best thing."

"No!"

Before Conley could reach him, Angelo had pulled out a gun, rested it against his own temple, and pulled the trigger. The deafening gunshot shattered the peaceful morning. Waves paused, the sun pulsed to a stop, and the explosion's echo filled a sudden vacuum. Then all at once hundreds of startled gulls complained and took flight as Ocean Park's Chief of Detectives Danny Angelo crumpled to the ground.

Conley fell to his knees and checked for a pulse. Slow, fading, done. He took one last look at what remained of his former partner's face, the man's lifeblood soaking into the sand above where a thick, dark head of hair should have been, turned his own face away, and retched.

Chapter Forty

Silver sleigh bells—three of them—lined a leather strap fastened to the door. Their jarring clang welcomed every customer to the Woodstock, Vermont diner on a busy Memorial Day weekend.

Conley lifted his coffee cup and the skin of his forearm pulled loose from the sticky counter. The waitress hurried by, moving so fast her bangs parted and bunched at the temples. She stuffed tips in an apron pocket with one hand and collected dirty plates with the other. He raised a finger.

"More coffee?" she said.

"No thanks, I'm good."

"What then?"

"I'm meeting a friend. She's late."

She crossed her arms. "This friend going to pay your check?"

"No, no." He read her nametag and unfolded a hundred-dollar bill on the counter. "Will this cover it, Holly?"

One eyebrow arched. "I can't break that."

"Not asking you to. Do you know a girl named Gina? She knows this area. We got split up and she doesn't own a phone. We agreed to meet here on Memorial Day."

She flattened her hands on the counter, fingertips just inches from the money.

"I don't know her, but he probably does." She pointed at an old man in a window booth. He was watching shoppers outside stream in and out of antique stores and gift shops, dressed in sweaters and jackets on this unusually chilly spring day. "Frenchy lived here his whole life, knows everybody." Her voice trailed off. When Conley turned back to the counter, his cup and the bill were gone, and Holly was pushing through the kitchen door. She froze, spun on her heel, and returned with an afterthought. Her eyes narrowed and the purple makeup underneath cracked.

"You go easy on Frenchy, Mister. He ain't well."

Conley left the stool and walked to the booth.

"Mind if I sit?"

The old man's wattle shook when he nodded. His nose was red and bulbous, and a baseball cap sat high on his head like a crown.

"Waitress thought you could help me," Conley said. "I'm looking for a girl named Gina."

The watery film around the man's rheumy, bloodshot eyes glistened like crystal balls. "I know."

"How could you know?"

"I know what waiting looks like." He raised his arm and flicked his fingers toward the bells. "You jump like a jackrabbit every time the door chimes. This Gina," he said, wiping the back of his wrist across his mouth. "Her last name Starbird?"

"Yes."

Frenchy's papery hand reached into his coat pocket and came back with a half pint of Bushmill's. He twisted the cap, poured a shot into the cup, and took a long pull.

"Makes Holly's coffee drinkable." He glanced

around and winked. "She don't need to know."

"'Course not. You said Starbird."

"I did. Pura must be 100 years old by now."

"I'm sorry to have to tell you, but he's dead."

The old man bowed his head and studied the table. An argument erupted in the kitchen. Holly's voice fired loud, staccato bursts. The deep voice that answered was just as quick and abrasive. She had the last word before a long silence.

Frenchy pocketed the bottle. "Pura dead? Hard to believe. He was a Magyar, y'know. Gypsy royalty. Used to pass through here regularly with those two kids—Gina and Luca—following the same route every year, right down to the day. Thought he'd never die."

"Do you know it? Do you know this route?"

"Me? No. If he ever told me, my memory ain't givin' it back."

The sleigh bells rang. Two women came in, arms full of shopping bags, and searched for a table.

"But I remember one of his pit stops—the one before he came here."

"Tell me."

"Slow down, sonny." Frenchy licked his putty-colored lips with a yellow tongue. "I'm gonna tell you the whole thing my way, logical-like. Then you can decide if you still want to meet up with a Starbird."

He laid his arms on the table, lifted his chin so his turkey neck straightened, and began.

"Lots of drift trade used to come here to work the tourists. I was in the DPW, made sure the hawkers obeyed city ordinances—parked where they should, didn't trash the place. Them Gypsies set up on the Commons for two weeks every summer, a big tribe with campers and vans. The men ran exhibitions—knife play, whips, juggling. Women sold potions, peddled aphrodisiacs, mood changers, all kinds of crap. The kids—Gina and Luca—sold sweet meat on a stick. I helped Pura a few times, talked the constable into cutting him slack. Those Gyps weren't hurting anybody, just trying to make a buck—even if it wasn't always an honest one."

"When was the last time you saw them?"

"I'm getting there." He drank from the cup, shuddered, and ran his open hand down his face.

"You might want to take it easy on that stuff," Conley offered.

"Don't worry about me. A lifetime of Lucky Strikes is fighting Irish whiskey for last rights to this old body. My money's on the smokes.

"Where was I? My friend Ruffin, he was there too. Me'n Ruff worked together most of our lives. I understood him, but many didn't. Hard man, never could leave well enough alone. Liked to be a prick. He'd cuff the little Gypsy children for no good reason, got an enjoyment only he could comprehend. Pura saw him do it once and I thought the Gyp would burn Ruffin's flesh with those shiny black eyes. I broke it up, got between 'em. Frenchy the peacemaker.

"But then things escalated. Pura used to arrange blood sport—dog fights, cock fights, and such—to gamble on. Held these battles down behind Thornton's barn, near the Queechee Gorge. Ruffin was a customer, always complained about the odds and payouts. Told me a lot of money changed hands, from his to someone else's. One night the pot went missing and winners didn't get paid. Pura got blamed, but he pinned it on ole' Ruff. Did the two of them ever have it out? Who knows?

"Ruffin disappeared soon after. Vanished. Rumor was he run off with a married woman, but I didn't buy it. Besides, none were missing. Police couldn't find him, not that they looked very hard. Wife and kids didn't seem to care much either, 'cept about the life insurance. Then one day someone spotted a piece of cloth on the steep embankment under the steel span bridge. Bright-colored rag, hard to miss. Ruffin wore those lumberjack-type shirts almost every day, so naturally, it set people thinkin'.

"No sense searching any further into the gorge. It was spring and the river at the bottom's a wild snake until June. If Ruffin had visited those rapids—that was the theory—there wouldn't be enough of him left to interest a turkey vulture."

Holly appeared, breathless, cheeks red, coffee pot in hand. "More high-test, Frenchy?"

"Just a splash, Beautiful."

A quick pour and she was gone. Frenchy spiked the cup with more whiskey and took a long draught before he continued.

"Y'know, I never believed those Gypsy magic stories—till I was in one."

He started coughing. Coffee gushed from his nose. Drops of blood splattered his shaking hands.

"Frenchy?" Holly called. "He bothering you?"

"Not as long as he's listening. Old men rarely get an audience, sweetheart. Leave him be."

Conley gently freed the bottle from the old man's grip and wrapped his own hands around it. "You've had enough, Frenchy. Go on, finish your story."

He shrugged and gazed toward the ceiling, as if he were reading text on the asbestos squares, and continued.

"The cops decided to lower me from the steel arch bridge into the gorge. I done a bit of rock climbing, knew how to rappel, so I drew the short straw—not that I remember anyone ever bunching straws in a fist.

"They made a rope harness—not a very good one—and squeezed me in. When they were tying me up, I asked for a smoke. Everyone smoked in those days to relieve the nerves.

"Suddenly there's Pura, passing me a hand-rolled, already lit. Funny thing about that butt—it had no smell to it. White smoke, burning tip, but when I took a drag it tasted like I was sucking dry steam.

"They lowered me, spinning in that hemp chair, sheer cliffs circling around me like a merry-go-round. I remember the bottom of the bridge, a rusty skeleton of steel grates. I could see right to the sky through the tiny grids. Cloudy day, barely any blue peeking through those gray suds. I looked down. The river was a white boil, running hard. Then I looked up again—I'll be damned if Pura wasn't helping the sheriff lower me. And that piece of checkered cloth waved in the breeze, beckoning like a racing flag. The rope was brittle and dry, and it started popping. Frayed strings stood at attention like cowlicks. I was more scared than I ever been, twirling in that damned truss."

His eyes glistened more.

"They lowered me farther, payed out rope fast like I was too heavy to hold, though I barely weighed a hundred pounds. I twirled, I jerked, and vertigo set in like I never experienced. Was it Pura's cigarette—or him dropping me so fast? I don't know. The wind picked up and swung me like a pendulum. I wanted to quit. Yelled as loud as I could, but nothin' came out. Couldn't move. I was paralyzed. When they finally swung me over to that flapping rag, I managed to reach out. My arm felt like it weighed a thousand pounds. I touched the cloth—it was Ruff's all right, but I'd never prove it. My frozen mitt just batted it free, and it floated off to God knows where."

Frenchy started coughing again, and this time his eyes bulged. Phlegm made his throat sound like a blender crushing ice. Suddenly Holly's cold, calloused hand clamped Conley's and wrestled the bottle away. She lifted Frenchy's cup, sniffed the liquid, and snarled.

"You liquored him up, you slimy bastard. Get out."

"No, wait."

"I'm calling the cops." She sped toward the kitchen and burst through the doors. He followed.

The silver doors opened to a silver kitchen. The air was thick with the smell of frying oil. Eggs sizzled on the grill and a blade hammered a chopping board. A cook looked up. He was dressed in white, with a cocked cap that almost covered his salt and pepper hair. Holly yelled.

"Call the Sheriff, Charlie. He tried to kill Frenchy."

The cook stepped forward. "Shut up, Holly. You can't come back here, pal."

Conley opened his wallet and fished out hundred dollar bills. He laid five on the counter.

"Keep your money," Holly screeched. Her lips quivered. "Call the cops."

"Whoa." The cook stepped around the corner and stared at the bills.

"I need five more minutes with the old man," Conley said.

The cook pulled on his chin. A pot on the stove boiled over, thick and foamy. Water hissed on the burners.

Conley placed more bills on the pile. Charlie wiped both hands on his soiled shirt and touched the money gingerly, as if it might burn. He lifted a bill, held it to the food warmer light, and ran his fingers across its middle.

"Are these real?"

"Yes."

"Real blood money," she snarled. "Don't do it, Charlie."

The sleigh bells chimed in the restaurant. The cook hooked his big hand around Holly's bicep, pulled her close, stuffed a bill in her apron pocket, the rest in his. He smiled at Conley, lifted the cleaver from the cutting board, and pointed its gleaming tip at the double doors.

"Your five minutes just started."

****

The van's hood opened with a creak and steam poured out. The hood strut was broken, so Luca found a branch and propped it against the engine block. Gina leaned over the fender, her shoulder touching his. She whispered, as if his quiet inspection were sacred.

"What's wrong?"

"Radiator leak."

"Can you fix it?"

"We'll see."

He opened the radiator cap with a rag and set it on the fender. He dabbed the grill with the cloth.

"Can we leave soon?"

He looked tired. Worry lines fanned from his eyes and mouth. "We'll see." He hopped into the van by the side door and returned with hands full. He cracked an egg on the lip of the radiator hole. The yolk oozed inside. Mustard seed next, poured from the bottom of his closed fist. The steam was dissipating, a low hiss. He added more, then retrieved a plastic bucket and headed toward the pond.

The clearing hadn't changed much. Pura had told her the fire road that led to it wasn't built for travel, but as a break in the forest to contain fires. The branches were overgrown now, almost touching, a green arch that shaded the rutted dirt road. She found Pura's tree, an ancient oak where he used to place her in its low crook so she could watch him forage. The trunk was shiny and smooth where he'd skinned bark for poultices. The tree's canopy shaded a glen filled with mushrooms fat and tall—brown, white, and mottled.

Luca returned, arm pulled straight by the full bucket of water he carried. He knelt and placed a clean rag over a second pail. He poured water through the cloth, reversed the buckets, did it again, then poured the water in the radiator opening.

"Pura loved this place," she said. "I think he loved being alone."

Luca replaced the cap, jumped onto the driver's seat, and called out the open window, "He was never alone. He always had us."

The engine came to life, then suddenly quit. Water sloshed through the hoses. He jumped out and inspected the radiator grill.

Another engine rumbled far down the fire road. Reflections sparkled through the branches, tires crunched faintly. She peered through the low-hanging canopy. Luca called her, his voice deep and worried.

"Gina, where are you going?"

He got in the van again, turned the ignition, and the starter whined.

"Gina, come back! We can go soon."

She kept on, still distraught about her missed appointment with Matt Conley, and what he must have thought when she wasn't at the diner. Would he look for her? Would he believe that a dying radiator was keeping them apart, or would he think she'd had a change of heart? The months they'd spent together were the best of her life, and now nothing was as important as being together. She longed, she ached, she felt physically ill at the thought of never seeing him again. Love's mountains were ecstasy, its valleys hell.

The faraway rumble grew louder, a steady hum. She stood in the middle of the road now, on the high part between the ruts. The branches overhead joined like clasping fingers.

Behind her, Luca cursed. The radiator groaned and whistled.

The car was almost through. Tree branches brushed its windshield.

Gina sent up a quick prayer—and prepared herself to see the face of the only man she hoped would be determined enough to find her in Pura's secret place.

A word about the author...

Mike Walsh attended Boston University, where he became a staffer for the *Daily Free Press* and earned a degree in journalism.

His first professional job was at a public relations and advertising firm, writing press releases that appeared in the *Boston Globe, Boston Herald,* and *New England Journal of Engineering.* He later became a technical writer, writing and editing jet engine manuals for General Electric Aircraft Engines.

He's written and studied fiction for years at BU, the University of Cincinnati, and now Jacksonville, where he won the First Coast Writers Festival short story contest and had work published in the UK's Twisted Tongue and Askew Reviews. He's an active member of the Bard Society, Florida's longest-running workshop.

His first novel, *Ocean Park*, began the mystery series about Detective Matt Conley and his struggles with crime and heartache in the New England city where he was born.

Mike and his wife Jean live in Florida with their three boys.

Thank you for purchasing
this publication of The Wild Rose Press, Inc.

If you enjoyed the story, we would appreciate your
letting others know by leaving a review.

For other wonderful stories,
please visit our on-line bookstore at
www.thewildrosepress.com.

For questions or more information
contact us at
info@thewildrosepress.com.

The Wild Rose Press, Inc.
www.thewildrosepress.com

Stay current with The Wild Rose Press, Inc.

Like us on Facebook

https://www.facebook.com/TheWildRosePress

And Follow us on Twitter
https://twitter.com/WildRosePress